Her Best Friend's Brother

T.J. Dell

For my husband, Daniel.

For believing in me,
And for giving me something to believe in.

Contents

Prologue

"These are good." Tony Marchetti stuffed one chocolate chip cookie into his mouth and scooped the last two cookies off the plate and into the front pocket of his shirt. "'anks, 'ibby," he mumbled at her as he strolled out of a sliding glass door with crumbs trailing behind him.

Libby McKay's whole face lit up and she beamed a grin after him for many long moments after she could no longer see him. Libby knew the cookies were good. Chocolate chip was Tony's favorite. Libby's mom owned a bakery, and she had taught Libby the secret to making the very best chocolate chip cookies. Libby had loved Tony for more than two years. And two years is a long time when you are nine years old.

Libby met Melanie Marchetti on the first day of second grade. Four days later, on a Friday night, Libby and Melanie took turns braiding each other's hair in front of the television with a big bowl of popcorn between them—in true slumber party fashion. The back door slammed, Libby turned around, and in walked a boy dressed head to toe in mud. Immediately he began to elbow out of his stained football jersey, and using the relatively clean underside of that jersey he swiped most of the mud and dirt from his face. Soft brown eyes appeared out from under the layer of dirt. Dark shaggy hair fell across his forehead. He toed off his shoes and carried them with him into the Marchetti laundry room. When he reappeared he was wearing fresh jeans, and a soft white tee shirt. His face and hair were damp, and still smeared as if all he had bothered to do as far as washing was splash a handful of water on his face.

All of this happened in about 45 seconds. And for 45 seconds Libby stared, with her mouth wide open, and without taking a breath.

"Who's this, Pigtails?" The boy rounded the couch, tugged on the ends of Melanie's painstakingly braided and styled hair, and plopped into the recliner across from them.

Mel's hair was exactly color Libby wished for herself: a pale silvery blond. Libby had carefully gathered it into one pretty French braid for her friend. Libby's own dark curls had been slightly more sloppily arranged in two braids. Not pigtails really, but all the same Libby quietly pulled them out, suddenly hating the childish hairstyle.

"Don't call me that!" Mel tossed a handful of popcorn at him. Lunging forward, he chomped at the air trying in vain to catch the kernels. "You would need *two* for pigtails! Libby, that's Tony— my brother. He always calls me that even though I haven't had pigtails since KINDEGARTEN!" The last word was yelled in her brother's direction.

"Every day of kindergarten," Tony chuckled as he brushed the popcorn off his shirt and strolled out of the room.

And that was all it took. Libby was in love. Not that she told Mel. She did have some pride, after all. Besides, Tony was 11 years old – and in middle school!

After that first week of school, Mel and Libby were rarely apart. They ate their lunches together in school, and they did their homework together at Mel's house after school. On Saturdays they alternated between playing in Mel's big back yard and playing at the park across from Libby's apartment building.

The first week of January, Mel and Libby celebrated their birthdays together at the ice skating rink. Mel's birthday was actually in December, but she didn't mind waiting for her party because no one wanted to go to a birthday party right before Christmas anyway. In June, when the Marchetti family spent a week in the outer banks, Libby was invited too, and in July, when Libby and her mom took a long weekend in Williamsburg, Mel tagged along. Of course, a week spent in the outer banks had the added benefit of Tony's company.

Nothing much changed in the third grade except Mel and Libby were forced to endure being in separate classes. They still traded sandwiches at lunch time, and they still watched The Little Mermaid every weekend, and Libby was still in love with Tony. And that's how it was year after year; Libby and Melanie were best friends and closer than sisters.

Chapter one

"It's red."

Libby stared into the three-way mirror in the dressing room. At sixteen she was beginning to like what she saw in the mirror. Her hair was still a plain dark brown, but Mel had spent the last summer experimenting with home hair dyes, and Libby reaped all the benefits with her almost expertly done low lights. Also over the last year, her figure had certainly blossomed. Mel's tall willowy frame was more stylish, but Libby secretly preferred her own curves. The red dress that hugged her full breasts and draped *just so* over the swell of her hips would have hung awkwardly on her friend.

"Red is not appropriate for a wedding."

Libby twisted slightly, admiring how the steep slit winked open, displaying one long leg.

"It's a Christmas wedding, Lib. I don't think those rules apply. Besides, it isn't really red—it's more of a wine." Mel sighed dramatically and flounced into a chair. "You can't really be considering putting it back. This dress was made for you. If anyone else were to wear it you could sue!"

"It's not exactly a one of a kind; there is a rack full of identical dresses waiting to drain other wallets of other girls." Libby was used to Mel's dramatics, but she still felt it was her duty to bring her friend's brain out of fashion magazines and back to earth every now and then. "And while it isn't haute couture, it also isn't exactly priced to move." Grimacing at the price tag, Libby mentally calculated how many batches of cookie dough she would need to slave over to cover the price of the dress.

Not that working at her mom's *Eat Your Heart Out Café and Bakery* was ever really slaving. She loved baking and it sure beat the retail job Mel was stuck with. That reminded her that Mel's lunch break was almost over and a decision must be made if she was going to take shameless advantage of her friend's employee discount. "Maybe I should try the pink one again?" She reached for the cocktail length dress chosen from the clearance rack.

"Absolutely not. This is a grown up event and that is a little girl's party dress!" Mel took a deep breath and started again in what she obviously thought was a casual tone. "Tony is flying in tonight.

Did I mention that? He decided he could use a break after his finals after all. And he didn't really want to miss Olivia's wedding anyway."

Libby's stomach turned over. "I thought he got a job for the winter break."

"He did. Some newspaper—something gazette, or herald, or … whatever. He doesn't start until Monday. Mom and Dad paid for his plane tickets, so he'll be here tonight, go to the wedding tomorrow, and fly back Sunday afternoon."

Actually, it was *The Examiner* in Trenton. He had rented a cheap apartment in New Jersey for the next two months and his salary would only just cover the rent, but he was so excited about the job he didn't care if he ended up losing money. That was why he hadn't originally planned on making it to his cousin's wedding. He was worried he would run out of cash and was hesitant to buy the tickets home. Of course, Libby couldn't exactly correct Mel. Because Melanie didn't exactly know that Libby had been talking to her brother lately. Well, not talking really, but they had been trading short emails, and there had been a few late night online chats.

It was mostly just silly stuff. It must be hard for him to be away from home and it wouldn't be very macho of him to be talking to his baby sister all the time, so Libby figured this was just his way of staying plugged into Taylorsville. It was such a small town they didn't even have their own *Examiner*. So it was hardly like he could get his home-sick-fix any other way.

Anyway, there really wasn't that much to say. A couple times a week she would get a thrill when she checked her email and saw *tmarchetti124@gmail.com* pop up in her inbox. It was never more than 3 or 4 lines. Usually about something silly in his day, or lately about how much more stressful exams were as a sophomore than last year. Sometimes he would ask her about her schoolwork, or about the bakery. Once he had sent her text message with a picture of a guy using an electric razor on the subway and the caption 'Only in NY. Gotta love it'. It was the only time he had ever texted her, and she shamelessly looked at that stupid photo approximately 12 times a day. It made her grin so uncontrollably that she was careful not to sneak any peeks when Mel was around. Twice when she'd been online later than was normal for her, *TMarchetti*: had popped up in a chat window over her email account. Both times they chatted for over an hour. Talking to him was so easy; especially online, because if she wasn't fighting the urge to swoon every time he smiled, the conversation didn't have any awkward pauses.

Tony was in the middle of his sophomore year at Columbia in New York. Libby knew he had recently decided on a journalism major. It made sense to her; Tony had a way with words. He always told the most bone chilling scary stories when they were kids.

"So will he be going to the wedding … with us?" Libby felt her face heat up and began concentrating on the hem of the gown in question. It was too humiliating that she couldn't even muster Mel's level of a false casual tone.

"He doesn't have a date if that's what you mean." Mel's grin split open behind her, but the mirror still gave Libby three horrifying views of it. "It's is about time he noticed you weren't a little girl anymore, and that dress will get the message across loud and clear."

"Don't be ridiculous, Mel." Libby blustered her denial even as she made the decision to buy the red gown. A girl was only young once, right? And she could put in some extra time at the bakery over Christmas break anyway.

"Please. You have been drooling over him for years. Not that I know why – you have seen his bedroom, right? The whole room ought to be condemned!"

"I don't make a habit of hanging out in your brother's room," Libby called from inside the dressing room where she was hurrying into her own clothes. It wasn't precisely true, but there were some things a girl couldn't share even with her best friend—especially if that girl was in love with her best friend's brother. "The red dress. You're right, it is perfect, and with your discount I can afford it."

"Good. I am pretty sure my lunch break was up like 4 minutes ago." Mel held out her arms for the dress as Libby emerged from the dressing room, and the girls headed for a cash register. "I'm not exactly glad that things with Cory didn't work out, but as far as dates go I could do worse than you." Mel linked arms with her best friend. The only reason Libby even had to spring for the stupid-beautiful-look-how-grown-up-I-am dress in the first place was because Mel and her boyfriend, Cory, had split up after Mel had RSVP'd a plus one. "I am glad you are going, you know. I don't know what you see in my slob of a brother, but you would be a way improvement over Miss Cat's Eye Glasses and Turtlenecks."

"Sorry, what?" With many years of practice, Libby was usually good at keeping up with Mel's flitting train of thought, but she was genuinely stumped now.

"Over Thanksgiving, when I went to visit Tony in New York, and I had the most amazing Christmas shopping trip. Got more for myself than anyone else on the list, but totally worth it. I do wish I had gone back for those boots…"

"Mel!"

"Right, sorry. When I went to visit him, this Stephanie girl was always hanging around. They have a bunch of English classes together I guess. She wore turtlenecks all the time. It isn't *that* cold in New York, and she wears cat's eye glasses. We are not talking retro look-how-cute-I-am-sunglasses. Oh no. These were full-on 1950s everyday eye-wear cat's eye glasses. They might as well have been on a lanyard!"

Okay, so the glasses thing was all Mel. Personally it mattered very little to Libby what sort of eye-wear a person preferred, but a girl? Hanging around with Tony? And he hadn't mentioned her… she would certainly have remembered that.

"So they are dating, but not go to a wedding with me dating, or not fly to North Carolina for a weekend with me, or…" Libby couldn't go on. It was too awful. Tony. Girl. Cat's eye glasses. Suddenly she completely agreed with Mel that 1950s eye glasses were obviously tacky.

"I don't know. I got the impression they had gone out a few times but it isn't like I found her name scrawled next to his on his school books or anything. He is going to love the dress. You know he and Olivia have never been very close. I didn't really think he minded missing out on the wedding, and then the other day I told him about Cory—and that you were my new date. Voila. Home for the weekend. Makes you think."

But all Libby was thinking of as she walked to her car with her bags was Little Miss Turtlenecks and her cat's eye glasses. Stephanie. She even had a stupid name. Actually, Libby had an aunt named Stephanie, and the name had never bothered her before. But she hadn't been thinking objectively then, and of course now she was all about objectiveness—right. It shouldn't matter. She knew Tony dated; she knew he'd had girlfriends. Some of those girlfriends had been to the Marchettis' for dinner on nights when Libby was also there. But now – well, was it her imagination that she and Tony had gotten closer lately? Certainly he hadn't ever emailed her last year while he was away at school, and then there had been all those late nights in his bedroom.

Last summer when Libby's mom had been invited to teach a two-week workshop at some pastry school in Pennsylvania, Libby spent 14 perfect days at the Marchettis' home. Not that she was glad when

Mel caught a nasty stomach bug the last 5 days of her visit, but she hadn't been in a hurry to turn Tony down when he offered to take the couch and give Libby his bed so she would stay germ free.

Tony had made a small attempt to clean up, and of course Mrs. Marchetti had changed the sheets, but it was still his room. His bed. His space. Just remembering gave her goose bumps. The Tuesday that Mel started feeling ill, the new sleeping arrangements were finalized and her things were moved to Tony's room by 7:00. That was too early for bed, but for the first time in eight years she had felt awkward and out of place in the Marchetti home. With the family room transformed into Tony's temporary bedroom, there weren't a lot of options. So she had changed into her pjs, borrowed a book from the family library, and settled nervously on top of Tony's twin bed to read and wait for sleepiness to claim her.

At first she almost didn't hear the knock at the door. But then came a louder knock. "Libby? You aren't asleep already, are you?" Tony's voice always gave her heart flutters but Libby forced herself to sound calm.

"No. Come on in. Is this okay?" Libby gestured, indicating where she was sitting on his bed.

"Of course." Tony pulled a face and shook his head at her. "We told you it was fine a million times. I don't mind the couch, really – Mom never let me have a TV in here anyway, and in the dorm I got used to falling asleep to Letterman's top ten. I just thought it was pretty early. In all the years I've known you I don't think I have ever seen you hit the sack before midnight."

"Well, I usually have very important and secret slumber party rituals to complete." Libby was relaxing more and finding that talking to Tony in her pjs, in his bedroom, wasn't all that different from talking to Tony anywhere else. Except that now she wasn't wearing a bra, and that had really started to matter lately. Shivering nervously, Libby looked around for a discreet way to cover herself.

Tony must have seen her shiver because he grabbed a blue hoodie off a hook on the back of the door, and tossed it to her. "Here … it can get chilly in here." He made himself a little busy straightening the frame holding his high school diploma on the wall for several seconds.

"Thanks." Libby shrugged into his sweatshirt, inhaling deeply the mix of his cologne and laundry detergent –a smell that was distinctly his.

When she looked up, Tony was looking at her a little strangely. "It is clean. I wore it for a few minutes yesterday, but only out to the mailbox and back. It's clean."

"Okay. It's clean." Now Libby almost thought Tony might have been the nervous one, but that was probably just her overactive imagination

Shaking off the weird moment, Tony produced a very battered Monopoly box from under his arm. "I thought we could play. Maybe it's time we had our own slumber party rituals." The last part was said with a teasing grin, and despite the fact that her heart was desperately trying to pound its way out of her chest, an easiness settled back over them. Tony sat cross legged at the foot of the bed and set up the board between them.

They played for hours, and talked the whole time. It was the first time Libby could remember having any lengthy conversation with Tony that didn't also include another member of the Marchetti clan. And they talked about a lot of stuff. First they debated the strategy behind great Monopoly players: green properties vs. blue (green obviously), and utilities vs. railroads (railroads if you could get all four of them were the better deal by far). Eventually the topics spun off and they were discussing life, and classes, and colleges. When Libby admitted she had tried out for cheerleading at the end of the school year, Tony laughed.

"You would make a terrible cheerleader."

"I wasn't that bad," Libby whispered practically too herself. She could jump and giggle as well as anyone else. Besides, she knew perfectly well that Tony had dated Ellen Kirkpatrick for months his senior year, and she had been the cheeriest of cheerleaders.

"Don't get all sullen on me, Libby." Tony chuckled and shook his head at her. "Every year you come over for the super bowl, and every year you make me explain the rules of football, and every year you fall asleep before it's over! That's the most exciting game of the year. No way you make it through a high school football game every Friday night for an entire season. No way."

"You might be right about that." Libby chewed on her lip as she counted out the price for Pacific Avenue. "I think I am going to try out for track and field. I like to run."

Tony stilled for a moment and raked his eyes over her the length of her body. "Yeah." His voice was a little huskier than normal. "I could see that. You definitely have the legs for it."

Just remembering the appraising way his eyes had settled on her legs where they were stretched out along the edge of his bed was enough that she could feel a blush rising to her cheeks.

Every now and then Tony would smile at her. Like when she told him that she remembered what a good storyteller he had been as a kid, and that journalism sounded like a good idea. It was not the *I love my life* easygoing Tony smile she was used to. It felt like a new only-for-Libby smile.

When Libby could no longer hold back her yawns they checked the time; it was actually early morning and Tony had long ago missed the Top Ten.

"Should we call it a draw? Or see who has the most cash?" Tony smiled slyly and Libby knew exactly what he was up to.

"No way, Marchetti! I have 3 monopolies! You might have more cash but a few more turns around the board and it will all be mine! Nothing doing – we can finish tomorrow."

"How do I know you won't cheat during the night?" Tony played along with mock outrage.

So they carefully wrote down who owned what and their cash totals, and they even went to the extreme of carrying the board to the garage and locking it inside. When the door was locked and the key solemnly slid underneath Mr. and Mrs.

Marchetti's bedroom door (for safekeeping), the hilarity of it all (compounded by the fact that it was now almost 2:00 in the morning) overtook them and they exploded into giggles. Giggles! Anthony Marchetti actually giggled!

Libby grinned at the memory.

When they caught their breath, Tony walked her back to her room – his room, really – and for one excruciatingly long moment things got weird again. Exciting weird. At the door to his room she turned to say goodnight, and found him only inches away from her. With one arm braced against the door frame over her shoulder, he leaned in and was so close she could almost taste his breath. It occurred to her that if she arched into him even a little bit she would feel his hard chest against her body. And after eight summers of beach vacations with him she had a true appreciation of his upper body.

"This was fun. You know, Libby, I think this is the first time we have ever played together. We should do it again." His voice went all husky and low. Was he flirting with her? No, he couldn't be—but still this was new.

"We can finish the game tomorrow, and we play Scrabble all the time at the beach." Scrabble was a Marchetti family vacation staple.

Tony looked almost confused for a moment, and then his smile returned. Not the only-for-Libby smile, but the old friendly smile.

"'Night, Lib." Tony straightened up, reached out to open the door behind her, and turned and walked down the hall. For one fantasy moment she had thought Tony had actually been about to kiss her. Even though she was exhausted, it took her a very long time to drift off to sleep that night, and she nearly slept through Mrs. Marchetti's huevos rancheros the next morning.

The next night, instead of sitting on the bed, Tony wheeled in his father's office chair. It made the small room even smaller, and Libby felt a certain loss at sitting on the bed alone. "I must be getting too old to sit up all night with no back support," Tony joked as he settled into the chair. For just one fleeting second she thought she saw him look sort of longingly at the empty space on the bed.

Monopoly lasted three more nights, with Tony holding on through stupid barters and desperate trades. Honestly, Libby purposely let him make those stupid barters just to drag out the game, but somehow she had the feeling that he knew what she was up to and he didn't seem to mind. Every now and then his voice would drop an octave and tease her in that new way that made her heart leap, but there were no more moments when she could taste his breath. No more *is he going to kiss me* goodnights. Each night they locked up the board as if it were the most important game of Monopoly in the history of games of Monopoly, and each night Libby lay awake far too long afterwards reliving each word and each smile.

On Friday night, Tony finally, albeit grudgingly, admitted his utter defeat in Monopoly. This seemed a little convenient since she was going home the next day.

"Libby?" Tony took a deep breath. "Libby, did you really like those stories I used to tell? When we were kids?"

"I don't know if *like* is the right word—since your sister and I would be awake for days afterwards, afraid to close our eyes… but… yeah. They were good."

"Did you know I used to write them down? Not just when we were kids, but I wrote a lot of stuff my last couple of years in high school. It would be cool, I think, if I wrote something people actually read. Not just a newspaper article that is going out with the recycling, but the kind of thing people kept on their shelves and read over again every once in a while."

"A book. Tony, you are talking about writing a book, and I think that is fantastic." Libby smiled wide and bright because she knew Tony was sharing something with her, and because she knew he could write a phenomenal book.

Tony smiled back. Her special just-for-Libby smile. "Yeah. A book. I want to write a book." He breathed out a deep sigh. "I think I could do it. A collection of short stories, or maybe I'll really go for broke and spin out a full length novel. A thriller. I love a good thriller, you know?" It all came out in a rush and Libby was so swept up in his excitement that she threw her arms around him and squealed.

"Go for it, Tony. Go for broke—it's gonna be great!" Less than a second later, Libby realized what she had done. And from her head to her toes she felt every inch of her skin come alive. Slowly, almost hesitantly, Tony's arms circled around her waist. He barely touched her at first, and then suddenly he tugged her against him in a tight hug. His hands splayed open across her back, pressing her torso to his. She had wanted to open her hands against his back, and feel the muscles she knew, from lots of careful observation, were there. But an instant later his hands were at her hips and he was setting her carefully away from him.

"Thanks, Lib." Without looking away from her, he reached over to his desk and pulled out a pretty battered spiral notebook. "Maybe you could read some of these. Just enough to tell me if they are any good. Really. I need you to be honest with me." Tony shoved the book at her. "The stuff at the back is the most recent. I know the grammar will need some work, but…" He was actually rambling. Tony Marchetti had lost his cool talking to her! Definitely a highlight of her life so far.

"Not tonight—since I am sure I wouldn't sleep, but as soon as the sun is up I would love to read these."

"Don't… this isn't public knowledge, okay? Mel doesn't need to know about this."

"Of course! I won't tell anyone." It rankled her that he felt the need to even say such a thing. This was clearly personal for him and not her business to be spreading around.

"I know you won't, Lib. You're a good friend." Softly, he leaned in and brushed his lips against her forehead. Her forehead! Like a child! But it was a kiss, and hope bloomed warm and bright in her heart.

And his stories really were great. Now that Libby was old enough not to let them give her bad dreams at night. That was how the email-pal bit had gotten started. With Mel no longer incapacitated it wasn't like Libby had a reason to have many private conversations with her brother. So she had started emailing him as she finished each story, and he would email her back. When she had read the last story there hadn't felt like a need to stop emailing him. And surely he would have let her know if she was starting to pester him—wouldn't he?

This was dumb. There was no reason for her to start second guessing herself now. They were closer than they used to be. She used to be his kid sister's best friend. And now she was his friend. As much as it pained her to hear him put her in the category of good-friend, at least she was in *a category*. She was not going to start second guessing herself now. And the dress was … perfect.

Chapter two

It was probably too much. No. She looked fantastic. Looking into the full length mirror in Mel's bedroom, Libby couldn't quite convince herself. Libby had spent more time getting ready that morning than Melanie did, and Mel was a bridesmaid! Of course, Mel had basically just stepped into the elegant gold shift style bridesmaid dress, clipped a few strategic locks of hair back, and applied a little make-up with practiced ease. It took about two minutes for Mel to look as though she had stepped out of one of her fashion magazines. Libby on the other hand had subjected herself to over an hour of fidgeting while Mel tucked and pinned and pulled her curls until they looked to be gathered effortlessly away from her face save for a few carefree strands that had *escaped*. Mel also did her make-up for her. The finished product looking back at her from the mirror was far more dramatic than Libby had envisioned, but she really did look fantastic. At 5'7", Libby tended to avoid heels, but she was glad Mel had insisted on the cute little spiky heels. And anyway, Tony was pretty tall—definitely over six feet.

"It isn't too much. And Tony is going to flip." Mel's reflection appeared behind her in the mirror. She had always been a little too good at reading Libby's expressions.

"No. I was just making sure everything was in place," Libby denied uselessly as she backed away from the mirror.

Further discussion was made blessedly impossible as there was someone knocking on the door.

"Are you two ready yet? For crying out loud, if we don't leave now we'll be late!" Tony's exasperated voice sounded from the other side of the door. Mel was supposed to be at the church early for bridal party photos and Tony was driving them over so that Mel could ride with the other girls in the limo after the ceremony. So while they weren't exactly late, they probably did need to leave.

"Hold onto your shirt, brother!" Mel hollered back as she handed Libby a beaded purse, and tucked her own clutch under her arm. "We have plenty of time, but let's go."

Mel pulled open the door and strolled down the stairs to the front door. Libby stalled before the doorway. She had never seen Tony in a suit and tie before. His normally shaggy hair was trimmed short, and while she loved to watch him habitually brush his hair out of his eyes, this new style made him look … well, like an adult. An incredibly hot adult. Libby took a moment to concentrate on not allowing her tongue to hang out of her mouth.

Tony took one look at her and let out a soft whistle. "Libby McKay… all grown up." Had he really just whistled at her? What should she say? Why was he staring at her that way? "Are you ready, Lib?" Tony crooked his elbow towards her and Libby realized that, of course—he was waiting for her to move forward. Silently, since she couldn't trust her voice, Libby tucked her hand under his arm and allowed herself to be led to the car.

At the church, Mel was whisked away for photos, leaving Libby and Tony with 45 minutes until the ceremony. He looked questioningly down at her feet. "Are those shoes okay for walking? Main Street is only one block that way. I thought we could take a walk and check out the Christmas window displays."

Ridiculously pleased that Tony had given any thought to spending time with her—even just a walk down Main Street—Libby replied, "The shoes are fine, but this wrap isn't exactly December appropriate." Libby pulled the thin wrap closer around her body, emphasizing that despite the mild evening there was still quite a chill in the air.

Tony nodded thoughtfully for half a moment and then wordlessly shrugged out of his wool pea coat and draped it over her shoulders. "Let's go." He touched his hand to her back and nudged her towards Main Street.

They walked quietly at first. Not touching, because Libby was just about swallowed up in Tony's coat, but still they walked side by side close enough for Libby to smell his cologne. After a few minutes of comfortable silence, Tony said, "So, still thinking about Track and Field in the spring?"

"Try-outs are right after winter break. I have been running most days at the indoor track at the Y. I like the distance runs the best. I'm working on my mile, but I am practicing sprints too."

"Does Mel go with you? Or someone else? It would probably help to have a coach with a stopwatch. I know Sam Tucker was pretty big into track back when I went to school there."

Sam Tucker was a senior, and he was on the track team. It surprised Libby that Tony would remember him since he would have been a sophomore when Tony was a senior. Sam and Libby had gone out a few times, including the homecoming dance a couple months earlier. They had a good time, but had both agreed that they weren't seriously interested in each other.

"I usually go pretty early, and you know Mel only wakes up early for important things… like sales. But I have an old stopwatch and can time myself, and I do okay."

"So Sam doesn't take you running?"

"Umm… no." Why were they talking about Sam Tucker? Talking about Sam was sort of killing the nice pseudo-date buzz Libby had going a moment ago.

Tony nodded and checked his watch. "We should probably start back if we want good seats." Tony slipped one arm around her waist and turned her around to head back towards the church.

"Hey, kid! Look up!" A man coming out of a shop door grinned and pointed up. Sure enough, hanging just over their heads from the awning in front of a consignment shop was a sprig of mistletoe.

The arm that Tony had innocently rested around her waist the moment before was now heavy and warm as he drew Libby closely into his chest. Tony dipped his face down to hers and whispered, "Merry Christmas, Lib," against her lips. Gently, he brushed his mouth against hers and then slowly and tenderly he was moving his lips with hers.

As kisses went it was relatively innocent. Not that Libby had a lot of experience, but there was no insistence, and no tongue. All the same, Libby felt her stomach flip over and all her bones seemed to want to melt away. Long before she was ready for it to end, someone let out a loud wolf whistle and Tony pulled away.

"We better hurry." Tony shoved his hands into his pockets and walked quickly half a step ahead of Libby all the way back to the church. Libby was left wondering if something had gone wrong. Personally she thought that was just about as perfect as a kiss could get, but again—she hadn't had a whole lot of experience.

He was being rude, he knew. But he walked faster anyway. The sooner they were surrounded by relatives, the easier keeping his hands to himself would be. And until then he made fists in his pockets—just in case. This was trouble. Libby was his baby sister's best friend, and he could probably be arrested for the thoughts he was having right now. But the way she looked tonight, he was having a very difficult time convincing his body that she was only 16. Sure, lately he had been thinking that they might be good together, but not for a few more years. Four years wouldn't seem like such a big difference when they were a little older. She was still a kid, for crying out loud. Of course, he had been younger than she was doing a hell of a lot more than some mistletoe kissing, but that was really not the point. Did she have any idea how she looked in that dress? She was basically walking sin. It covered much more than any of the swimsuits he had seen her wear year after year, and for that matter it covered more than those skimpy pajama shorts he had been tortured by last summer. And yet somehow it was much more… shall we say *effective*.

When they reached the steps to the church, Tony slowed down and fell back into step beside Libby. "Looks like we made it in time."

"With plenty of time to spare, too."

Libby seemed a little miffed with him. Although he had been very rude most of the walk back here, so he probably deserved it. Libby lifted the hem of her dress slightly as she climbed the steps. And that scandalous skirt fell open, revealing one long perfect leg clear up to her slim, toned thigh. Tony stifled a groan.

They should have had to ask for ID before selling her that dress. It was a wonder she had time to buy a dress at all let alone find one so…. A horrible thought took root in his brain. Her invite to the wedding had been terribly last minute. Maybe she hadn't had time buy a new dress. Homecoming couldn't have been more than 8 or so weeks ago. Maybe that was what the dress from. Mel had been annoyingly vocal about how cute Libby and Sam looked together at the dance. It was possible Libby had bought this siren's dress for Sam Tucker. That particular thought came with a punch to his gut. Sam Tucker, with his sleek black truck and tinted windows. There was only one good reason for a teenage boy to have tinted windows. The very thought of Sam Tucker seeing Libby, his Libby, in this dress made Tony so angry he couldn't think.

"Have I told you how much I like your dress?" Tony leaned over to whisper in Libby's ear when they were settled in a pew waiting for the ceremony to start.

"You whistled at me before we left." Libby couldn't help her teasing smile. "I'd say that translates to *like*. I haven't ever been whistled at before."

Tony decided not to mention that 15 minutes ago a stranger had whistled at her when she was in his arms under the mistletoe. He took a deep breath and tried again. It was suddenly very important that he know if Libby had worn this beautiful dress for Sam Tucker. "I guess Mel was lucky you could get a dress on such short notice. Or maybe you already had it— from homecoming or something?"

"Homecoming? This would have been way overboard for a homecoming dance. Mel picked it out yesterday actually, and she lent me her store discount."

"That's good." Sounding genuinely pleased, Tony relaxed into his seat and draped one arm across the back of the pew.

The wedding was very beautiful. And if anyone had asked her the details of the ceremony later, Libby would have had nothing to say. You see, it was basically impossible to concentrate on anything other than Tony's warm arm on the back of her seat, and how the tips of his fingers would occasionally brush against her bare shoulder, sending bolts of electricity through her nervous system.

There weren't a lot of options for elegant affairs in Taylorsville, but there was very nice hotel in the center of town with a big ball room, and that is where they headed for the reception. Mel of course rode over in the limo with the bridal party, so Tony and Libby rode together in his car. And that pseudo-date feeling snuck its way back into Libby's head. Libby had been on a few dates, but 'date-talk' was pointless between her and Tony since they already knew each other inside and out. That didn't mean that they rode in awkward silence though. There was always an easiness between them. Even when they were silent it was never really truly awkward.

"I have decided to start compiling an anthology of short stories. I have some new ideas, and with a little work a few of my older pieces could really be something." They were discussing his writing. He talked passionately about his creative writing professor, and about a writing group he had joined that was full of peer critiques which were apparently tremendously helpful. Libby smiled and listened. This was how she liked Tony: full of excitement and plans, and sure of himself. This was her Tony. "I haven't given up on a real novel though. I have a hundred ideas. I am leaning towards a detective series. Thrillers. Real bestseller list stuff, but I think getting my feet wet with some short stories is smart."

Tony guided his car into a spot at the hotel. "I'm boring you aren't I?" He said it with humor, but there was sincerity too. He hadn't meant to ramble on and he didn't have many private moments with Libby, and now their 15 minute car ride was over and she hadn't gotten a word in edgewise.

"You never bore me." Libby giggled softly at the very idea of being bored and being with Tony at the same time. "Will I get to read it?"

And there it was, that only-for-Libby smile. Tony covered her hand with his. "You will be the very first. I promise."

It was a perfect night. Everywhere she looked, Libby was charmed by the silver and gold Christmas themed decorations. Of course, she was seated with Marchetti family, but it didn't escape her that she ended up in the chair next to Tony rather than the one next to her *date*, Mel. They were served a beautiful fancy meal with more forks than she had any idea what to do with, but she could hardly feel uncomfortable sharing a meal with the Marchettis. No matter what the trappings.

When the band started to play, Great Aunt Somebody-Or-Another came and stole the family away for photos. Even then, when she was left alone at the table, smiling dumbly at her goblet of ice water, she still didn't have any time to feel awkward. Because the minute Tony's arm left the back of her chair she had plenty of attention. She danced once with one of the groom's friends, but he stepped on her toes and his hand was a little too low on her back. So she was happy to oblige when Mel's cousin Nick cut in. Nick was probably two years younger than her, but he kept his hands to himself and he was a good dancer. Besides, he confided in her that he had been stuck at a *kids' table*. And if there was anything Libby could sympathize with it was being labeled as a *kid*. After laughing with Nick through the electric slide, Libby found herself with Frankie.

Frankie Marchetti was one of many, many Marchetti cousins, but Libby had met him once or twice before when she tagged along to family functions. She thought he was maybe one year older than Tony, and he was very good looking. He was tall like Tony was, but with a darker complexion and slightly too beefy muscles. Frankie was from one of the more Italian branches of the family tree. He was a good dancer even if he did hold her a little too close.

"So. Little Libby… all grown up." His head started to bend towards her, and panic seized control of Libby's brain, making her step backwards. Frankie's words were so close to what Tony had said, and yet they made her stomach lurch in a very different way.

"Sorry. It's so warm in here I think I will get a drink." Libby walked away quickly.

At the bar, everyone in front of her was leaving with a glass of champagne, and Libby had just about made up her mind to order one for herself when Tony's hand closed around her elbow.

"Cherry Coke… extra cherries, and champagne for myself." Tony spoke smoothly to the bartender, but his eyes narrowed when he steered her back to their table. "Do you drink now?" he accused her.

"How do you know I wasn't going to order the Cherry Coke?" Libby bristled at her abrupt return to *kid sister* status.

"You wear your every thought on your face. If you were a little older I would love to play poker with you."

Libby jerked her elbow out of his grasp. "I am old enough, thank you very much." Although at this point it was anybody's guess as to what she was *old enough* for. "And you are hardly a stellar example. What would you have done if they had carded you for that glass of champagne?"

Tony arched a brow in her direction. "I would have shown him my ID," he answered wryly.

"Don't be ridiculous. You are only 20."

"I have an ID that says otherwise," Tony murmured as they settled themselves back at their still empty table.

"Well, well. Pot, meet kettle," Libby muttered, more to herself than to Tony.

"Come on, Lib. There is a difference. You are 16! I will be 21 this summer."

"I'll be 17 in two weeks." Now Libby was really talking to herself as she felt the last of her pseudo-date buzz slip away.

"And is 17 old enough to make out with my somewhat skeazy cousin Frank?" Tony was whispering now, but every word was laced with anger and disapproval. So that was it. Tony felt he had to rescue little Libby McKay from his big bad wolf of a cousin. "He has a girlfriend. And how would Sam Tucker feel about you draping yourself around Frank?"

Again with Sam Tucker. For Pete's sake, they had been on three lousy dates and shared one lousy kiss. Big emphasis on the LOUSY. "I did not make out with Frankie. We danced to two songs. Then I got warm so I decided to get a drink and sit down." She didn't add that sitting down had actually been Tony's idea. No point in reminding him of that. "And Sam Tucker wouldn't have any reason to give a damn one way or another even if I left with Frankie."

"Which you are NOT going to do!" Tony was so shocked by her words he knocked over the glass of champagne. Not that he really wanted it—he had been more trying to make a point by ordering it.

"Which I am not going to do," Libby agreed easily. "Just like I did not make out with him."

"He kissed you," Tony hissed, although more calmly since reason was now settling back into place in his brain. "And why wouldn't Sam care?"

"We aren't a couple, Tony. We went out a few times, but it was nothing. And Frank *almost* kissed me. I walked away, but I guess you missed that part while you were busy rescuing me from myself. Not that any of that is your business. I have been kissed before. I am not a little girl."

Sam wasn't her boyfriend. Libby didn't have a boyfriend. Wait, who had she been kissing? "Who have you been kissing?"

"Again, not your business. But I do believe I kissed you earlier today."

"And here I thought I was the one who kissed you." And just like that, things were okay again. Tony had seen red when he came looking for Libby and saw her so close to Frank that he doubted a piece of paper could have passed between them and he thought he saw them kiss. But he could have been wrong about that. And Libby was here now. And she wasn't dating Sam Tucker. "I'm sorry, Lib. I was… well, I had a weird moment, but I'm better now."

There it was—her just-for-Libby smile. So she wasn't angry anymore. "How did the photos go?" she tried to change topics.

Tony grinned. "They took forever! All those moms and aunts and grandmas and great aunts and no one knew what was going on or who should stand where. It was a mess. Remind me, when the time comes, to elope!" For just a moment his last words hung in the air between them, taking on a slightly different meaning than he had intended. Wow—did the air sizzle and snap! Leaning in, Tony touched her arm. "Dance with me, Libby."

When they danced, Tony held her close. Not pressing against her the way Frankie had, but he gently tugged her into him and tucked her head under his chin. "You smell like lavender."

"It's lotion. I have dry skin."

Tony chuckled. Only Libby could make having dry skin sound so sexy. "You smell great. I love it." A few heartbeats passed before Tony spoke again. "Did I tell you Olivia's college roommate, Tara, pinched my ass during the photos?"

"What!" Libby laughed at the conversation change and pulled back a little to look him in the eyes.

"She did! I felt like a piece of meat. It was disgusting." A smile quirked at the edge of his mouth. "And she is headed right for us." Tony leaned down and whispered in her ear, "Let's you and I pretend we are here together—on a real date."

"What?" Libby breathed out the word even as her heart skipped.

"Please? It will chase Tara away." His breath was warm and moist on the shell of her ear.

"'Kay." She turned to look at him, but his face was only an inch away from hers. He wasted no time in closing that distance. This was no gentle mistletoe kiss.

His lips molded firmly to hers. His tongue swept over lips and she opened, willing him to deepen the kiss.

"*Tony*!" A high pitched, sugar sweet, sing-song voice invaded their moment. "I hope you are saving a dance for me." The woman was a few years older than Tony and a blond bombshell that filled out her bridesmaid dress like she had gotten it a size too small—on purpose.

"Tara." Tony turned, keeping his arm around Libby. "I don't believe you have met my date—Libby McKay." His voice was easy, but not warm. Tara did not take the hint.

"Your date?" Tara looked confused for a moment, but she recovered quickly. "Libby. Oh right, Libby. Aren't you little Melanie's *date*?"

"Does it look like I am on a date with Mel?" Sliding her free arm across Tony's chest until it rested just inside his suit jacket, Libby angled her body into his. Libby was not going to be intimidated, and she sure as hell wasn't giving up on a date with Tony Marchetti – even if it was a pretend date.

"Well, I guess I will see you two around." Tara turned around, looking a little dazed, and headed towards the bar.

"You were amazing!" Tony spun Libby back into his arms, laughing. "Is she still watching?"

Libby had no idea where Tara was. "Yes," she answered immediately.

"Good." Tony drew her into another deep kiss. Angling his mouth over hers, this kiss shook her all the way to her toes, and as he backed away he softly whispered, "Wow."

Every minute of that night was forever burned into Libby's memories. Most of her dances belonged to Tony, and he even presented her with a glass of champagne when it was time for the toasts. All too soon the evening was over, and Tony was dropping her off at home. She hoped he would walk her to the door and maybe she would even get another kiss.

"I had fun, Lib." Tony cocked a grin at her as he pulled up in front of her building.

"Me too."

"Well, have a great Christmas. I won't be home again for awhile. I have an early flight out tomorrow and I start at the *Examiner* the next day. But I'll be in touch." And he said the whole thing smiling. Libby couldn't believe it. The best night of her life and a dress worth an entire winter break of servitude to her mother's bakery and *he would be in touch.*

"Great. Thanks for the ride. Merry Christmas."

She climbed out of the car. Her apartment was on the fourth floor. For the first two flights she was determined to be angry with him. But by the time she finished climbing the last two flights she was determined to be positive. It had been a great night. And he did say that he had fun. By the time she fell asleep that night she was sure that Tony Marchetti was one step closer to realizing he couldn't live without her.

Chapter Three

Merry Christmas! It was so weird to miss Christmas with the fam, but plane tickets home would have been worth way more than my sorry ass makes in a month. I love it though. Not that I ever get to do anything important, but it's a real newspaper. You know? I talked to Mom and Dad and Mel earlier. It sounds like they had a good holiday. My across-the-hall neighbor and I went out for Chinese. It sounds lame but it was kind of cool.

I thought about calling you, but I didn't know when you'd be busy. So, Merry Christmas, Libby. I hope it was a good one.

-t-

Chinese sounds good. You know me and my mom—we ate so many Christmas cookies that neither of us could eat the Turkey dinner we made. So we had turkey pot pie for lunch today. I saw your family yesterday. I stopped by for a little while. They missed you—even Mel.

I missed you too.

-L-

A few days later a box came in the mail for Libby. Inside she found a digital runner's stopwatch. A little handheld thing that had settings for keeping track of her best times, and trends, and other things she hadn't even known she needed to track. It was the most thoughtful gift. And Libby liked it almost as much as the card she found enclosed. It was a plain holiday card with a drawing of mistletoe on the front, and inside Tony had scrawled a note in this barely decipherable writing.

Thought this would come in handy. Lots of luck. Love, Tony.

Love. Not Sincerely, and not Yours Truly. No, Tony had signed Love. Of course, boys probably didn't think very much about these sorts of things, so Libby tried very hard not to read too much into it. But that didn't mean that she didn't do a happy dance around her bedroom after tucking the card into the frame of her dresser's mirror.

Just got your package. I love it. It is perfect. Tryouts are in two weeks so keep your fingers crossed for me!

-L-

How did it go?

-t-

I'm so in! They post the official results tomorrow, but I had the fastest mile. Not the fastest mile for a girl. I had the fastest OVERALL mile! Just shows what a good stopwatch will do for training.

-L-

Not five minutes after she hit send, she got a thrill from the message box's 'ping'.

TMarchetti: That's great! Congrats.

Libbylibbylibby: Thanks. I am super excited about this. I have never played any sports before. At first I just wanted to have an extracurricular for my college apps this summer, but now I totally want to win.

TMarchetti: That's great, Lib. You sound happy. I'm sure it was all you, but I am glad you liked the stopwatch.

They chatted about nothing in particular for almost 45 minutes. Libby floated into her bed that night. Every couple of days she had come to expect an email or a text from Tony. Nothing particularly special or personal in content, but he always made her smile, and occasionally he had her laughing so hard her eyes would water.

A week or so later she got a birthday card in the mail, and it joined her Christmas card in a place of honor above her dresser. That was their pattern. Light and occasionally slightly flirtatious pen pals. It meant the world to Libby, but sometimes she had to wonder what, if anything, it meant to him.

Happy Birthday, Lib. Mel says you are going to a movie? That sounds awfully tame for one of your parties! Do you remember the year when you two dragged us to The Little Mermaid on Ice? *You were so disappointed in Prince What's-his-Name. I hope you have fun.*

   -t-

It was Prince Eric! And the actor was all wrong. The movie was fun. I guess we have just outgrown princesses and ice shows.

   -L-

Wow. All state! Mel was so excited for you she barely spent any time talking about prom dress shopping. I was more interested in your news anyways. Why didn't you tell me last week when we talked?

-t-

Well, I am pretty excited, but I figured I would wait and see how I actually place before I got all braggy about it. I didn't want to have to tell you if I came in last – it would be too awful.

-L-

You're dumb. That better be the last time you ever worry about having to tell me anything. Besides, no way are you coming in last place. I wish I could make it home for the all state meet, but I really need all the study time I can get.

-t-

"Sam Tucker asked you to prom?" Mel was out of breath as she ran into the bakery. "And you said NO!"

"Really, Mel, who is your informant? It hasn't been more than an hour." Sam had asked her right after school let out, and now 45 minutes later Mel was already *in the know.* "He wasn't upset; it was more of an I-don't-have-a-date-you-don't-have-a-date sorta thing."

Mel pulled a face. "You could have a date. I know you aren't interested in Sam that way, but he is way hot and a good dancer. And at least you could go to the PROM!" Her eyes narrowed as Libby concentrated on arranging a tray of cup cakes. "You do want to go, don't you? You haven't been out with anyone in ages. Actually, not since Christmas. Is this still about Tony?"

She could feel the color rushing to her cheeks. "No. I just haven't been out. What's the big deal? I have been way busy with training and the bakery." Libby kept her eyes down and tried to keep her voice even and normal. A distraction. She needed a distraction to keep Mel's mind away from Libby's non-relationship with Tony. "So, Cory, huh? Are you sure you want to go there again?"

Cory and Mel had the whole school talking at least once every six weeks. Were they together?

Were they broken up? Did you hear about their fight in homeroom? Libby was more than a little convinced that the notoriety was a part of – or even all of – the attraction for her friend. And, much to Libby's displeasure, Mel rarely missed out on an opportunity to dissect their dysfunctional relationship.

Mel flicked her wrist dismissively. "He's a bit of a bad habit with me, but he is a great dancer, and he makes me laugh. Besides, he is going to look great in pictures…" Her eyes widened. "You are changing the subject!"

"I am not."

"Last month you told me you had had it with all things Cory and you were boycotting all future references to him and to our relationship. Am I supposed to believe you have suddenly regained interest?"

"Last month I had to drive across town to pick you up from that party at like midnight because you refused to let him take you home."

"Hello! He was practically drooling on Sherri Munski. I was so humiliated and…STOP! This is not going to work. We have got to talk." Mel wiggled a little on the stool at the counter as if to settle in. "I know I kind of encouraged you at Christmas, but that was when I thought Tony was going to come to his senses." She took a deep breath. "And I don't think he is." She waited for that to sink in.

"He kissed me." Libby hoped her words came out as nonchalant as possible.

"I saw. At the wedding. And that looked like some kiss." Mel's face twitched thoughtfully. "I think he's too old for you."

???? "When did you decide this? He is only three and a half years older. What happened to '*Make him see you as a grown up*'?"

"Well… That is hardly going to happen if you sit around at home every weekend!" Mel shifted uncomfortably. "Effie has been hanging around a lot lately. I think she is spending the summer in New Jersey with him when he goes back to *The Herald*."

"*Examiner*," Libby corrected absently. "Who's Effie?"

"You remember I told you about her before the wedding. Cat's eye glasses, always cold?"

"You said her name was Stephanie. What kind of a name is Effie?" Geez—how many girls was she competing with? Not that she was actually in the competition, because she was in North Carolina and he—well, he wasn't.

"Did I?" Mel didn't seem overly concerned about that detail. Mel wasn't really a detail kind of person. "I must have been mixed up. It's Effie. I think she's Greek, or Italian, or something."

This just got better and better. Exotic, probably had an accent, and she was obviously smart. They would hardly let dummies in at Columbia.

"He didn't mention it to you? In any of his emails?"

Libby froze. "What do you mean?" Mel didn't know about the emails. Unless Tony told her. Was Tony talking to Mel about her? Did she want him to?

"Don't play dumb, Lib. He emails you all the time, right? And you were texting him all through the movie last weekend. I think we might have to watch something else tonight. It's possible I am actually outgrowing *The Little Mermaid*. Well, maybe we can just fast forward to the songs."

She had been texting him during the movie. Maybe she could have been a bit sneakier about it, but who has time for sneaky when Tony Marchetti needed her help in a crisis? Libby smiled at the memory.

Tony: whats the difference in salted or unsalted butter?

Libby: one has salt

Libby: why

Tony: I am baking cookies.

Libby: ???????

Tony: Ive seen you do it 1000 times! I am sure I can handle it. Salted or unsalted?

Libby: unsalted… you know you can buy cookies right? Premade and everything

Tony: I want to smell them baking!

***

Tony: It burned and the inside is still raw

Libby: I am almost afraid to ask … it?

Tony: The cookie

Tony: I made one big cookie

Tony: Are you still there?

Libby: Sorry I was laughing so hard Mel kicked me out of the room you probably needed a lower temp   did you at least enjoy the smell?

Tony: No it was different but I am eating the middle with a spoon now... not bad

Libby: you could get sick eating raw cookies!

Tony: after all that trouble I went to? I am willing to risk it

The next day Libby had packed up a dozen of his favorite chocolate chip cookies and shipped them off to Tony.

Okay, so Mel might have figured out the texts were from her brother. "He told you he emails me?"

"Duh—Lib. I figured it out. He knows more about what's going on in your life than I do these days. But that isn't my point. If you, for some reason I will never comprehend, want to be buddies with Tony, then fine. But please stop moping around the house waiting for him! I have all this teen angst and you are making me deal with it alone." Mel smiled to show she was, mostly, joking.

"So, tell me about Effie," Libby sighed resignedly.

"Not much to tell, but they are moving in together." There was a long pause while Mel seemed to be waiting for a reaction. She was so not going to get one. "You understand what I am saying, right?"

"Duh, Mel." Libby smiled halfheartedly. Maybe she should go to prom. "I think I am going to call Sam."

Mel grinned, and turned to saunter out the door.

Happy end of school. I bet you are really looking forward to having the summer off. How does it feel to be a senior?

-t-

Thanks. You too. Except I guess you won't be having the whole summer off since you are working again. Are you looking forward to New Jersey?

-L-

Libby knew she shouldn't be fishing. But if Tony was her friend, why wouldn't he want to tell her about his *living arrangements*?

Yeah I guess I am probably done with summer vacations. Just wait though; when you get a little older you kinda would rather work than lay on the beach.

-T-

A little older my ass! Libby didn't write him back for three days.

Chapter four

"We missed you at the beach this year, big brother." Mel had a phone wedged between her shoulder and ear as she chose her first day of school outfit. "You would have liked John and Parker. They were staying in the Johnsons' house next door. They are at NYU."

"You know interns don't get vacation time, Mel. I am sure you enjoyed having a chance to win at Scrabble with me gone. Are John and Parker the Johnsons' kids?"

"No, they were just renters. They were there all week. John is so into me."

"What happened to Cory?" Tony could really care less about Cory, but he did like to check in with Mel every now and then. Whether or not his baby sister had a boyfriend and that boyfriend's name was probably something he should know.

"Pish. Cory is old news. He hardly called me at all over the summer, you know. John calls me all the time. He and Parker even came out to spend the fourth of July with me and Libby."

That got his attention. "Parker is visiting Libby?" Did that sound casual and offhand? Maybe he should have asked about John first. "Umm, so you like John … hmm?"

"Yes to both. Libby was seeing Sam Tucker, but I think she likes Parker better. We went to the park and had a picnic before the fireworks."

"Sam Tucker!" Okay, that was not offhand. But he had been taken by surprise.

"Yes. Sam Tucker, the guy who actually asks her out on dates. You know what they are, right? Or don't you and Effie go out on dates?"

"It isn't like that with Effie. We were working in the same town, and it saved on rent."

"In a one bedroom apartment?"

"There is a pull-out couch. Tell me about Parker… and John." He did not have to explain himself to Mel. Effie was just his friend. Well, maybe more than a friend. But Effie wasn't looking to get serious any more than he was, and how could he justify casual sex to his baby sister!?

"Parker and John spent the weekend at the hotel in town and went back to New York the next week. Parker is pre-law, but John is going to be a doctor. I think that is so noble, don't you?"

Tony tuned her out. It was pretty obvious he wasn't going to get any more information about this Parker character, or about Sam Tucker. Not that it really mattered. Libby could date whoever she wanted. After all, he had spent most of the summer with Effie. And she should be dating. Isn't that part of the reason he hadn't put any pressure on her? He wanted her to have all the experiences of being a teenager, and that included dating. If he remembered correctly (and it wasn't *that* long ago), it included a lot of dating.

It snowed today. October is early for snow even in New York, but I was glad. Snow always makes me think of home. How many snowball fights have we had over the years? Mel would always chicken out and go inside for hot cocoa, but you were more of a trooper.

I wish I could show you New York. Especially in the snow.

-T-

I do love the snow. Maybe we'll get lucky and have a white Christmas. It has been years since I can remember snow at Christmas.

Mel is throwing a Halloween party this weekend. I am going as Velma… like from Scooby Doo. It isn't my first choice, but there are four of us. It was John's idea. So naturally he is Freddie, and Mel gets to be Daphne. But I don't mind being Velma too much since she is so excited.

-L-

I always liked Velma. I have kind of a thing for brainy chicks.

-t-

Of course he didn't have to ask who the fourth was. Mel had already told him that John and Parker were going to be in town for the party. Maybe he would try and make it too. Halloween would probably be the last time he had to spare before he needed to buckle down for finals. And he had something he wanted to show Libby anyway.

Tony couldn't help grinning to himself. Now that the decision was made he couldn't wait to get home. He hadn't been home in almost a year, and his whole body hummed with excitement at the idea of the trip. A last minute flight would not be cheap, but he had some money saved and he had the code to his parents' frequent flyer miles account. Wouldn't Libby be surprised to see him? Not that he was just going to see Libby. He missed his mom and dad, and of course Mel too. And Libby. He missed Libby. He wanted to see her in that Velma costume, and he most certainly didn't want Parker to see her in it.

Libby woke up, and her bed was spinning in circles. No, that couldn't be possible. On second thought it must be her head that was spinning. She tried to call out for her mom, but it would seem that some time during the night she had swallowed a basketball. Her throat felt tight and scratchy. Crap. She was sick. She would have to miss Mel's party tonight, and Parker's visit. Although she wasn't so much worried about missing him, as she felt bad for leaving him alone at a party where he wouldn't know anyone. Hopefully Mel would take the time to introduce him around before she crawled into a dark corner with John. The two of them weren't exactly discreet.

By the afternoon, and after some hefty doses of Dayquil, Libby was feeling marginally better. Not really well enough to go to the party, but the room was staying still, and she had found the energy to finish her English paper. When she had warmed her voice up a bit she was able to call Mel and rasp out an explanation. Mel was disappointed, but John had already arrived so Libby was confident that she would cheer up soon enough.

After a shower that, she imagined, washed away all her germs, Libby changed into fresh clean pajamas and climbed back into bed, determined to sleep off the rest of this awful day. And then the doorbell rang. Libby had not hung the 'Trick-or-Treaters Welcome' sign provided by their building manager, but not all kids paid attention to that sort of thing when free candy was at stake.

The doorbell rang again. Libby contemplated dragging herself to the door, and wondered if there were any candy decorations left from the cupcakes she had made for Mel's party. Maybe she could just hand out the cupcakes? They were just going to waste now anyway.

"Are you crazy?!" Tony's head popped around the corner into her bedroom. Had she progressed to full-on hallucinations? Tony. Here. In her bedroom? Yep, definitely hallucinating. "Under the mat? Who keeps a key under the mat? That is the first place anyone would look. Robbers, axe murders, escaped convicts… I can't believe you would be so careless."

Okay, this was not how her Tony-in-my-bedroom hallucinations usually went. Libby decided he must really be real. "I guess it isn't that unbelievable—you obviously looked there." Tony shot her a less than forgiving look. "It's fine, Tony. You have been living in New York too long. No one is going to bother us. Besides, we have a doorman. Any axe-murdering ex-convicts looking to rip off my mom's new Cuisinart mixer would have to get by the doorman."

That earned her a smile. "Yeah, Arthur would be a big deterrent. He was half asleep in front of a portable television when I walked in." Arthur was probably 200 years old and didn't actually open the door anymore so much as he waved absently as people let themselves in and out. That was probably why he had transferred to the night shift when Libby was a little girl. "Where's your mom? You shouldn't be alone when you're sick."

"Midnight Madness." Libby shifted into a sitting position. Tony nodded. He remembered now that the week of Halloween was also the Fall Midnight Madness. Twice a year the shops on Main

Street all stayed open until 1:00 am and hosted a kind of a block party—only with shopping. "She stayed home this morning, but she didn't want to ask anyone else to give up their Halloween night. Besides, I think she has something going with Stuart from the theater next to the bakery. Why are you here?"

Tony took a few steps closer. "I had some time before exams, and I thought I would drop in on the party. Mel said you were sick. Mom made you soup." Tony lifted an armful of packages that Libby hadn't noticed he was carrying. His eyes seemed to travel from the top of her head to where she sat cross legged under her pink flowered comforter. "Your hair is wet." He took another step towards her.

"I just got out of the shower. That is a lot of soup."

Tony stopped. Libby with wet hair. Libby in the shower. Water rushing down... No. He was not going to think about Libby in the shower. He took a few breaths and forced a friendly smile. "I brought more than soup. I will be right back." He turned and jogged out of her room.

Two minutes later he came back empty handed and swept a quick look around her room. Libby silently thanked the powers that be for Wednesday's spontaneous cleaning episode. And she prayed that she had remembered to put the lid down on her hamper. Dirty laundry was never a part of her Tony-in-my-bedroom hallucinations.

"This isn't going to work." Tony quickly closed the distance to her bedside, and in one motion scooped her (pink comforter and all) into his arms. Her arms instinctively wrapped around his neck as he carried her down the hall into the family room. Somewhere at the edge of her mind she dimly recognized that while this did happen in her hallucinations, he was usually carrying her in the other direction. Tony gently put her down on the couch, and left the room again.

When he came back he was carrying two bowls, and had a couple bottles of water wedged under his arm. "Dinner is served." He pulled their coffee table closer to the sofa and placed a bowl of chicken noodle soup in front of each of them. "I hope you don't mind. I helped myself. I love my mother's soup." He cocked a happy grin at her as she scrambled to edge of the couch to take a taste.

Libby took two big spoonfuls and sighed happily. "Mmm. Me too. What's in the rest of the bags?"

Tony watched her eat... stupid spoon. Maybe he should have brought a thermos. Was chicken noodle the kind of soup you could drink from a thermos? Tony didn't think so, and anyway, somehow he doubted that Libby drinking out of a thermos would be any less… effective… than watching her lick that damn spoon.

"Tony?"

"What? Oh, right, the bags. Well, we have a selection of DVDs, and—well, I have a surprise for you—for later."

Libby twitched her eyebrows at the mention of a 'surprise', but she pulled the bag of DVDs towards her and poked through it. He had brought a bunch of slasher films (probably in honor of the holiday), the first Pirates movie (probably in honor of the fact that he thought Keira Knightley was a babe), and… "The Little Mermaid?"

"I figured if you were sick and missing a party then I could make a cinematic concession." And there was that grin again. Libby was having a hard time deciding if it was the flu or Tony's smiles that kept giving her waves of light headedness. "So? What's your pleasure?"

Pleasure? Oh, the movie. "I will spare you on The Little Mermaid, but only because my throat hurts too much to sing along. How about Pirates?"

"You got it." Tony was relieved, and disappointed. When he had been tossing choices into the bag, those slasher films had conjured images of Libby clinging to his hand, burying her head in his shoulder and leaping into his lap. She had the flu for crying out loud. A gentleman would not be thinking what he was thinking. Really he had just wanted to cheer her up. And to be honest, arriving home in time to find a bunch teenagers dancing around his backyard in costumes, his sister plastered all over pre-med John, and no Libby, had been more than a little disappointing. So when his mother had asked him to bring the soup over he had ignored her annoying wink and hustled himself over to see Libby.

When the soup was gone and Johnny Depp was on his way to adventure on the high seas, Tony turned to Libby. "Is that Parker fellow going to mind you watching a movie with me, or Sam Tucker?"

"You have a weird obsession with Sam Tucker. What about Effie?" Libby dodged the question. It was true that she was supposed to be on a date with Parker right now. But that was more of a matter of default due to their best friends being make-out buddies than anything else.

"Effie isn't my girlfriend, Lib." Tony sounded agitated, as though he was tired of answering that question. This was categorically unfair as Libby went out of her way to completely ignore her existence.

"We were friends who were rooming together, and I have hardly seen her since we moved back to campus." Not that it was her business, but it suddenly seemed important to Tony that Libby understand. "I don't have a girlfriend at the moment."

His words reverberated in the air for a little while. Libby could almost feel the electricity zinging between them. She opened her mouth to say something and—she sneezed a loud and somehow hilarious sneeze. They were both laughing uncontrollably, and Libby was trying to catch her breath. It was amazing that even though the delicious tension from a moment ago had disappeared, Libby was still having the time of her life.

"I'll get you some tissues. I should have thought of that." Tony was still chuckling as he unfolded himself from his corner of the couch. "Do you need anything else?"

"Actually, the Nyquil is over the sink if you don't mind bringing it to me." Nyquil usually knocked Libby out, but she knew she had taken the last of the daytime stuff, and she didn't want to risk another sneeze like that in front of Tony.

As Tony walked down her hallway, Libby allowed herself a long look. Tony was wearing a blue Columbia tee shirt and old washed-soft blue jeans. Most guys, you wouldn't even notice their pants unless they were yellow plaid or something else equally odd. Tony made denim look good. It was his thighs, she decided. She could see the toned muscles flexing as he walked. And his tee shirt fit snuggly across his broad shoulders. Tony had played football for as long as Libby had known him. Even at college he had a group of buddies she knew that got together for a pickup game at least once a week. All those years on the football field had done Tony's upper body good. He wasn't bulky like some football players, but lean and broad with upper arms that strained slightly at his sleeves. She loved those arms.

When Tony came back and after Libby had dutifully swallowed her medicine, he settled himself onto the couch, draped one strong muscled arm around Libby's shoulders, and leaned back to watch the movie.

Libby tried to fight the effects of her cold medicine, but long before the hero got his girl she was slumped over onto Tony's shoulder and sleeping deeply.

Tony considered carrying her to her room, but he couldn't bring himself to do it. And anyway, her mother wouldn't be home for hours, and what if Libby needed someone? So he leaned back into the arm of the couch, and pulled Libby, still wrapped in her blanket, into his chest. It was getting late and he concentrated on matching his breathing with the rise and fall of her back until he too drifted off to sleep.

The next morning, Libby woke up in her own bed and felt as if she had never slept better in all her life. It took her awhile to focus, and then she remembered Tony visiting, bringing her soup and a movie. She also had a fuzzy memory of Tony wrapping her in his arms and snuggling her close to him, but that part was probably a dream. There was no way that her mom, at 5 foot nothing, could possibly have gotten Libby from the couch into her bed, and that left Libby with one thrilling option for how she had gotten back into bed last night.

Sitting up, she found a thick blue folder at the foot of her bed. Opening it, she found a note scrawled in Tony's familiar messy writing.

Libby,

Your mom is back, and I have to get home. I am leaving you the first completed draft of my book. I did promise you could be the first to read it, remember? Take a look when you get chance. I hope you like it.

Love,

Tony

Ps: In case you were worried—Johnny Depp gets away and Orlando Bloom gets the girl.

So that was her surprise. Libby grinned widely as she settled back into her pillows and began to read.

Chapter Five

"We did it!" Mel was jumping up and down and squealing her very best squeal. The pale green graduation gown bounced lightly as Mel did her dance. Pale green looked wonderful against Mel's blond hair and fair skin.

John picked Melanie up and spun her around in a circle.

"Congrats, babe!" he said, before wrapping her in a slightly inappropriate embrace. They were so ridiculously cute together. "You too, Libster." John shot her with a finger gun. God, she hated that nickname.

Parker pressed a kiss to the top of Libby's head. "Yeah. Congrats," he whispered. Libby really wished he would stop doing stuff like that. John and Mel had been together for awhile now, and inevitably Libby always ended up paired with Parker. Not that she minded; it had actually been nice that she could count on having a date for all the major social events of her senior year. And she really liked Parker. He was funny and confident, and while she hated to admit to being shallow, having a man fly in from his New York college to see her had lent her a certain amount of prestige. Mostly they got along great, and while they had shared a few lukewarm kisses, he hadn't seemed to be interested in much more. But lately he had been calling more, and always seemed to be touching her a little more than was necessary. Libby knew that with high school behind her she was ready to take the Tony Marchetti situation into her own hands. So the Parker thing could get awkward.

The Marchetti backyard looked beautiful. Paper lanterns hung from wires that Mr. Marchetti had strung between the trees, and Tiki torches dotted the edge of the yard. Mel had spent months planning her Hawaiian graduation party. Judging from the size of the crowd, it was a big hit. A big white rented tent sheltered lots of tables and chairs, but extra lawn chairs had been arranged all over the yard to accommodate the guest list. Libby had played the good hostess to Parker most of the night so far, but she was grateful when Parker got caught up in a conversation about baseball and she could slip away.

Libby wandered the edge of the yard, feeling a little chilly in her grass skirt and bikini top. But no way was she changing until Tony arrived. She knew she looked good, and she figured a little sex appeal could only help her cause. Tony's flight had been delayed and he had had to miss the ceremony, but she thought he would have been here by now.

"Do I get to hug the graduate?" As if she had summoned him with her thoughts, Tony's warm voice called from the edge of the yard. Walking towards his voice and letting her eyes adjust to the dark, she found him stretched out on an old lounge chair under a tree.

"I didn't know you had arrived."

"I've been here for about an hour. You were... busy." Tony stood up as she approached and scooped her up until she was on her tiptoes hugging him. His skin was hot against hers, and she could feel his breath warm and wet on her neck. He pulled her tighter for a long moment and then set her back down. "How does it feel?"

"Good." Libby breathed her answer before she realized Tony was probably talking about graduation. "It's great. I feel great."

Tony pulled Libby to sit down next to him on the lounge chair. He left his hand covering hers in between them.

"So, have you decided on a school? Time is running out."

Libby grinned. She had great news for Tony. "Actually, I heard back from Columbia, and I am in!"

Libby had been accepted just about everywhere she had applied. But she had been wait listed at her first choice—Columbia. Florida State had really impressed her the most and offered the best financial aid, but she wanted to be in New York. If she hadn't made it past the extra interview at Columbia and gotten off their wait list, then she had NYU as a backup school. But none of that mattered now. She was going to Columbia with Tony.

"Wow, congrats. That wait list is hard to beat. But is that where you really want to be? You sounded so excited about Florida."

"Well, I want to be in New York, so it was probably going to be NYU if not Columbia." Libby's smile dropped a little. In her mind this had gone differently. Tony should have swept her into his arms and proclaimed his joy that they could finally be together by now.

NYU. With Parker. Tony hoped that Libby wouldn't be able to see him grimace in the dark. When Libby had first applied to Columbia, Tony's mind had gone into overdrive imagining being with her. But she had really been excited after she met with the people from Florida, and he only had one year left in New York. He had even been toying with the idea of moving down there after graduation— assuming Libby was amenable to the idea. One more year, he told himself. Let Libby spend a little time in college. A semester or two out of high school, and surely they could be together then. Of course, that was before he walked into this god-awful party. He had spent hours waiting at the airport, and he had still missed the graduation. Walking into the party tonight he had no trouble finding Libby.

She looked incredible in her luau costume. There were plenty of other girls here dressed in similar get-ups. Hell, he had even seen someone walking around with a coconut bra! But only Libby could get his heart rate jumping like that—of course she was the first thing he saw. The second thing he saw was that jackass Parker trailing behind her, always with his hand on her back or an arm around her waist. Of course, he had known they were seeing each other, but he hadn't realized Parker would be at the party. Foolishly Tony had been assuming he was going to be Libby's date, and just imagine how it felt when he realized Libby already had a date.

"New York is great, Libby; I just remember how excited you were about Florida. You even had me thinking of spending some time down there in the sunshine."

Libby was confused, but undeterred. Tonight was their night, she was sure of it. She scooted a little closer to him and moved her hand to his thigh. "I want to come to New York. You are in New York." Going all out, Libby wrapped her arms around his neck and pressed a kiss to his mouth. She hadn't kissed Tony in a year and a half. Not since his cousin's wedding. She was not disappointed.

Any chill she had been feeling earlier in the evening disappeared immediately. Her skin was on fire. His mouth was insistent and firm on her own, his tongue was sliding against hers, and unlike the kisses of her memory she no longer felt he was holding back. Tony wrapped one arm around her waist and dragged her closer to him. Groaning into her mouth at the feel of her breasts crushed against his chest, he tunneled his other hand into the hair at the nape of her neck, tilting her face for a deeper kiss. Encouraged by his reaction, Libby dragged her hands between their bodies and with shaking fingers she began to undo his shirt buttons. All she could think of was touching him, feeling his skin beneath her fingers, tracing those muscles she had spent years studying. His hands joined hers and for one fleeting moment she thought he was going to help her find that skin she was so desperate to feel. But then he closed his fists over her wrists and pulled out of their kiss so abruptly that Libby was pretty sure she whimpered her protest.

"Libby. Stop. What are you doing?"

"I told you. I want to be with you." Libby tried to lean in again and resume the kiss, but Tony held her in place.

"We can't do this, Lib. Not now. Not like this." Tony tried to keep his voice calm. All the while his body was screaming its objections.

Libby recoiled from him, humiliation settling in her chest. "You don't want me? You don't want to be with me?"

"Of course I want you! Where were you three seconds ago? You are so beautiful. You are the most stunning thing I have ever seen. Dressed the way you are tonight, every man at this party wants you—I can't help but want you, but that isn't to say … we aren't… together..." Tony stumbled trying to explain. He had a plan. Why was she messing with the plan? Why wouldn't his brain pull it together so he could make sense out of all this? Only, he knew why—it was because most of his blood had drained southward the moment she had touched his leg.

"But that's it? That was just your physical reaction to the way I look?" Libby scooted further away, snatching her hands back.

"Christ, Libby! It isn't like that." Frustrated in more than one way, Tony dragged his hand through his hair. "You're seventeen!"

"Eighteen." Libby chewed on her lip.

Tony's eyes narrowed on her. "Mel is seventeen."

"My birthday is in January, hers is in December. I am almost a year older." Libby's whisper was barely audible, because it took all her remaining energy to keep from crying. Had she ever felt so small?

Tony nodded. He knew that—he just hadn't been thinking clearly. "Eighteen. Okay, but you still just graduated high school. I don't know if the actual number makes a difference. And—not now, Libby. I can't do this with you."

Libby nodded. She couldn't trust her voice.

"What about Parker? For crying out loud, Lib—you are here with someone else. I am not about to snake another man's date." Now Tony was just talking. He thought if he could keep talking then he could take the pain out of her eyes. If he could keep talking he just might be able to convince himself he was doing the right thing.

"It isn't like that." Libby's voice shook slightly.

"Lib. He's here like once a month. Do you have any idea what it costs to fly to and from New York? Trust me—it's like that." Libby started to walk away. "Wait. Let's just... Can we talk? We're still friends...we can go back to when you first walked back here..." Tony jogged after her until she spun on her heels to face him again.

"I'm sorry, Tony. I think I have neglected my date long enough."

Libby turned and fled back to the party as fast as she could. Tony was left dumbfounded, staring after her. Eventually he headed back towards the house, angry and hurt and lonely and wishing he was still stuck in that damn airport.

Libby focused on being angry. Angry that Tony could flirt with her and kiss her and touch her and not really want to be with her. Angry that she wasn't enough. Angry that she had wasted her time on him. Angry that she had ever thought they could be more than pen pals. Angry was better than sad.

Better than devastated. Better than that lump of insecurity she felt growing heavy in her stomach. She found Parker easily enough in a crowd of guys still discussing some sport or another. Pulling him along with her, Libby went straight into the house and into Mel's empty bedroom. She didn't have a clear idea of what she was doing. It just suddenly seemed paramount that she prove, at least to herself, that she was a desirable woman. So she kissed him.

Parker kissed back. Expertly. He parted her lips with his tongue, he drew her hips into his, and he trailed his fingers up and down her spine. Libby's heart sank straight to the floor. "Wait." She pulled away.

"It's okay," Parker whispered, pulling her back and trailing kisses down her throat. "I'm prepared." What was he talking about... Oh! The meaning of his words sank in and snapped Libby back to reality.

"No," she said, taking another step back. "I'm sorry. This was a mistake. I know it was my idea, but..." She let the sentence trail into nothing, because she didn't have an excuse. Tony was at least right about this. She had treated Parker terribly.

"Hey. It's alright, Libby. We don't have to do this. To be honest, I was pretty surprised. I mean, I have thought about it, us more than casually dating, especially since it looks like you will be at NYU with me next year. But it's not the end of the world and, well—at least now we know."

Well, that decided it. No way could she be at NYU with Parker next year. Florida State wins... hands down. "I am sorry, Parker; I don't know what I was thinking."

"Stop apologizing, Libby. Just friends. That's cool." He pulled her back towards him, but it was a light friendly hug, and Libby really needed a friend. "So, friend, can I ask you a favor?" Libby looked up at him. "John and Mel left in our rental car about an hour ago... so..."

"So you need a ride to your hotel?" Libby smiled at her friend. "Come on, I need to get out of here anyway." Parker threw a companionable arm around Libby and pressed a light reassuring kiss to her temple as they headed for the front door.

"Parker?"

"Hmm?"

"How much does it cost to fly down here?"

Parker barked out a laugh. "Just a little humiliation." Libby must have looked confused because after they were settled in the car, Parker explained. "John's grandfather owns an airline. You know, corporate charters, but John works off the price of his flights, mostly as an air steward, and it doesn't cost the old man anything extra if I tag along—so really it only costs John a little humiliation."

"An air steward? Like a flight attendant?"

"Yeah, except the old man is kind of old fashioned. He prefers *air steward*, and since that term makes John turn red as an apple I have to say I like it too." They shared a good laugh, and Libby was satisfied that her friend hadn't been spending next year's tuition on plane tickets.

She was leaving. With Parker. Tony stood slack jawed in the hallway. He had come to find her and to beg her for another chance. He was such an idiot. She had offered him everything he had wanted for what seemed like forever, and he had thrown it all back in her face. All because he was a little uncomfortable with her age. They could have worked it out—maybe started slowly. He could have taken her on dates. Isn't that what Mel had said he should do? He could have taken her to Broadway, and the empire state building. But never in a million years had he expected to find her wrapped around Parker and headed out the door. It was probably his fault. He had driven her into someone else's arms, but that didn't take away the sting.

Chapter Six

They promoted me this year. Instead of coffee bitch, now I actually get to write something! Just the obits, but my name will be in next week's issue. And I get to send the interns out for coffee.

I am so sorry about everything.

-t-

How's Florida? It is already getting cold here, and I am thinking of you warm and tanned, basking in sunshine.

I hope you are enjoying school. Mel tells me you like going to class—naturally she is appalled. I think she is planning on majoring in parties at NC State.

-T-

Mel says you made the cross country track team. That's great, Lib. I know that must make you happy.

I know how busy you are, but maybe you could just let me know how you're doing?

-T-

One of my short stories was run in a local literary magazine. I wanted to send you a copy, but Mel won't give me your address. She says she thinks you're mad at me. I know she's right.

PS: Maybe you could give me an idea of how to make you less mad?

-t-

This year for Halloween I am thinking of renting an apple costume and riding the subway all day. You see, I used to get such a kick out of the characters I would meet on the train that I think it is only fair I give back to the community.

PS: I miss you like crazy, Lib.

-t-

I heard a joke today and thought of you… Where do cookies sleep? …. Do you give up? Okay, I will tell you. A cookie sleeps under the cookie sheets.

-t-

For the first time in almost five months, Tony had made Libby smile. She was tired of ignoring him, and tired of feeling humiliated. It was hardly his fault. Besides, as it turned out she was really happy at Florida State. So… she clicked reply.

That was so lame! You know why the cookie went to the doctor, right? Because he was a little bit nuts.

I do love school. I am making lots of friends, and I miss you too.

-L-

What did the big bucket say to the little bucket? ---------------------- You look a little pail!

Sorry, my baked goods humor is limited.

Thank you.

-t-

Happy as she was, Libby struggled to feel wholly comfortable in Florida. She knew of course that college would be different than high school, but knowing and experiencing were two very different things. Libby and her roommate, Suzy, threw themselves into campus activities. There were parties, and trips to St. George Island, and Libby had quite fallen in love with cross country running. She missed Mel, and her other friends, but there was a freedom in not being surrounded by people she had known since she was six years old.

At Thanksgiving, Mel flew down to Tallahassee, and Libby went home for Christmas and spring break. John and Parker had visited at Christmas too. Seeing Parker again was more pleasant than Libby had imagined. Perhaps, she thought, she was coming to terms with that awful party. Maybe this is what closure felt like. Closure was good, because Libby was quite certain that she could not go on waiting for Tony to love her back.

As Tony and Libby eased back into their friendship, both avoiding all mention of Mel's graduation party, they were careful to keep things light and friendly. Libby was determined not to miss his flirty teasing, because of course she knew, now, that those moments weren't leading anywhere she wanted to go.

They still wrote and texted and they had the occasionally telephone call. Once he even convinced her to try and talk him through baking cookies again. Unfortunately they got very involved in debating the latest John Grisham novel, and Libby's sincere belief that Mr. Grisham was the exception to the rule of the book being better than the movie. Some things just translate better on the big screen. Nicholas Sparks was that way too, but Tony declined to comment on Mr. Sparks, stating that no respectable man had ever sat through *The Notebook*, let alone read the book. But he said it in a way that made Libby suspected he had indeed seen the movie, and perhaps even read the book. They weren't able to agree on a conclusion regarding John Grisham, however, because the forgotten cookies had burnt up, smoking Tony right out of the apartment. Libby seriously considered sending him a replacement batch of cookies, but she was unwilling to risk falling back into old and unhealthy habits with him again.

After the last of her final exams, Libby turned, slowly surveying her now basically empty dorm room. Suzy had left the night before so one whole side of their tiny room was barren. The other side was piled with boxes to be loaded into the small U-Haul she was picking up in the morning. How strange, she thought—to be going home in the morning. Actually, make that later this morning, Libby mused as she noticed the time: it was after 2:00 am. She was excited to see Mel, and her mom, and even Stuart, her mom's boyfriend. But still it felt a bit strange to think of staying in her old bedroom in the apartment again.

The phone rang, shaking Libby out of her reverie. Tony's name blinked on her caller ID. He had graduated from Columbia that afternoon. Libby flipped her phone open.

"Congratulations! How did it go?"

"It was great. The whole family was there. Lot of photos. Very embarrassing. How did you know it was me?

"I have caller ID. Why do you sound weird?" Tony was talking too fast, and he sounded strange.

"That would be because I am drunk." Drunk! Tony didn't get drunk; at least, she didn't think he did. But she supposed that at 22 and after four years of college this probably was not his first foray into adult beverages. "The family left hours ago; the guys and I have been celebrating. I'm home now. In my apartment I mean, not home in North Carolina. I wish you could have been here, Lib."

Libby chuckled quietly. Tony drunk was just as charming as Tony sober. "I wish I had been too, but I had a late exam. I'll be home tomorrow night. Home in North Carolina."

"Why are you still awake?"

Libby laughed loudly at that. "You're awake too! I was just going to bed, actually. I had more packing left than I thought, and then I needed a shower, and then I got a phone call!" There was a long pause. "Tony? Are you still there?"

"Yeah, I'm here." His voice sounded a little deeper and thicker than before. "I interrupted you between the shower and your bed?"

"Umm, yeah. But don't worry about it." Man, he was weird sometimes. "Tony? Hello?"

"Still here, Lib. Just trying to decide if I am drunk enough."

"Drunk enough for what?"

"Tell me what you are wearing."

Libby's heart leapt. This was definitely not in line with their new, if unspoken, rules of engagement.

She would put a stop to it. Tell him to take his tipsy butt to bed and sleep it off.

"A towel. I am wrapped in a red bath towel." What had made her say that? Except it was true, but she hadn't really meant to tell him.

"I like red. Is your hair still wet?"

"Umm, yeah?" Was wet hair sexy?

"I have dreams of you with your hair wet wearing a pink blanket." Yep, apparently wet hair was sexy.

"You dream about me?"

"Will you get into the bed?"

"The towel will make the sheets wet." Libby was surprised he could hear her voice over the sound of her heart pounding.

"You could always take the towel off." She could hear Tony's breath with each word.

Tingles danced across her skin at the thought of him picturing her slipping the towel off and climbing between her sheets. "That does seem to be the sensible solution."

"Libby?"

"Yes, Tony?"

"I wish I was drunker."

What the hell? Wow he really sucked at this. "Wow, you really suck at this."

Tony laughed loud and warm, and the sound gave her more tingles.

"Sorry, Lib. And here I thought I was being so smooth." He paused. "I was out of my mind last summer, Libby. I couldn't take it if you cut me out again. I need you in my life and this is a bad idea."

"You're right." Libby sighed, but she was sure that in the morning she would be glad he had a called a stop to things. "I wish you were drunker too." That earned her a groan.

"Are you in the bed?"

"Yes."

"Pull the covers up, Lib. Close your eyes. Take a deep breath." Libby did as she was told. "Go to sleep, Libby. Goodnight." And then he hung up.

Libby threw her phone across the room.

Chapter Seven

"You're dropping out!" Libby felt bad that she had just announced Mel's less than excellent news to everyone in the bakery. "What are your parents going to say?" Mel and Libby had been all but inseparable over the summer, and while Libby knew Mel wasn't exactly looking forward to the start of classes, she certainly hadn't expected this.

"They already know, Libby! They agree with me. I am not exactly the collegiate type, you know. And if I withdraw now they can get a most of their tuition back. I'm not an idiot; I have given this a lot of thought. If you promise to actually listen I will explain it to you."

Libby felt bad for yelling. "Of course."

"Do you remember the tie I made for John last spring when Frank got married?"

Mel's cousin Frankie had gotten married the spring before. Melanie had found what she proclaimed was the perfect dress in the perfect shade of lilac, but she had been extremely disappointed when John hadn't been able to find a tie that matched her dress. This had seemed, to Libby, a tad ridiculous—but that was just Mel's way. So, Mel had taken it upon herself to make John a tie that went perfectly with her dress.

"John got so many compliments on it, and a couple of his frat brothers even offered to buy it off him. Not that he would sell it, of course. When his fraternity threw their end of the year formal, I designed at least a dozen new ties for them. Mom and Dad agreed to loan me the amount the college refunds them for this year's tuition, and I am going to move in with John in New York."

Libby was reasonably sure that some piece of vital information had been lost somewhere, but years of patience had taught her how to coax the information out of her friend. "Okay. So what is the money for?"

"Supplies, silly."

Okay, maybe she was little out of practice. Libby silently counted to ten. "What sort of supplies?"

"Oh, mostly silks, and some satins. And I will need a better sewing machine. And John has a friend that is going to set up a website for me, so I will have to pay him…"

"You are quitting school to make neckties?"

"Not just neckties. Scarves, and pocket hankies. And I am looking into a leather working class to decide if I want to try my hand at belts. I am starting with men's accessories because I think there is more room in that market. Plus John's mom is a surgeon and she promised to talk me up to her surgeon friends, and most of them are men. When the brand gets going I would like to do something with women's accessories."

"You're moving to New York!"

"Catch up, Libby." Mel's was smiling again. "I love John, and I am tired of only having one weekend a month together. It's going to be great. You are in Florida most of the time anyway. We can probably see each other even more with John's airline hook-up. I want to do this, Libby. I finally found something I am good at."

"You are good at lots of things." Libby chewed on her bottom lip while she processed everything Mel had said. "I think it's great, but you might want to take some business classes, design classes. Make sure you are really prepared to succeed." That was Libby's plan anyway. She wanted her degree in business so she could open her own café and bakery.

"Nah. I am kind of making this up as I go. Tony has a friend in law school that can probably point me in the right direction while I am getting set up. But now that I figured out what I want to do I don't want to wait another three years to get started!"

Libby nodded dumbly. "When did this happen?"

"Weren't you listening? My cousin got married and…"

"Not that, Mel. I was actually talking to myself. I was just wondering when I got left behind. You are going to be in New York with your career, and Tony is in New Jersey with his career, and I am left behind."

"Geez! Pity party much?" Mel tossed her crumpled napkin at Libby. "You aren't left behind; you are going back to Florida next week, and you have lots of friends there, and you actually like school. Libby, I was miserable last year. You were in Tallahassee, and John was in New York. Can you please try and be happy for me? "

"I am, Mel. If I were a man I would buy all my neckwear from you."

"Okay, good. Now that that is settled— do you want to help me move? John and Parker are going to be here tomorrow morning, and we are renting a truck and driving back. You could spend the weekend. Parker is."

"I'd love to, Mel, but I have a lot to do before Monday. I will come by in the morning and help you pack though." Libby wanted to say yes. That she would love to help Mel move, and see the fabulous town house where John lived. But she needed to start back to Florida on Monday, and Tony was going to be home for the weekend. He had told her so himself.

"Well, I suppose I should have given you more notice." Melanie seemed to be studying Libby's face. She blew her bangs out of her face and started talking again. "Tony is coming home tomorrow night." Libby wasn't sure how to respond, so she decided to play it cool and ignore her nosy interfering friend. Mel was completely undiscouraged. "You never really told me what happened with Parker."

"What? Nothing happened with Parker. We went out those few times with you and John, and now we are just friends."

"And with Tony?"

"Nothing ever happened with him either. We are just friends. It is better this way. You were right; he is too old for me anyway."

Mel nodded thoughtfully. "So you aren't going to tell me what you fought about last year?"

"Parker and I never fight. We get along really well." Libby purposely misinterpreted her question.

Mel nodded again. "Maybe you're right. Maybe you are being left behind a little bit, but you are doing it to yourself. When was the last time you went out on a date, Libby?"

Libby sighed in surrender. For the first time in twelve years, Mel was obsessing on someone else's love life. She had really crappy timing. "I go out, Mel. As you just pointed out, I do live in Florida, so that is where I do the majority of my going out."

Relief spread across Mel's face. "Okay! So dish. Who are we dating?"

Damn. "Well, it isn't serious, but Brian and I spent a lot of time together last semester." That wasn't exactly a lie. Brian had sacrificed most of his Thursday nights helping her pass freshman accounting. And it wasn't serious, mostly, because Brian was hopelessly devoted to his girlfriend. Not that she was disappointed, seeing as Brian was a bit dull. He would probably make a brilliant accountant one day, but he was still dull.

They chatted a little longer with Libby being as diplomatic as possible when the topic of Brian came up. When Mel hopped up and announced she was going home to pack, Libby was glad to have some time alone with her thoughts. She needed to think. It wasn't enough that she wasn't in love with Tony anymore, which she wasn't. Mel was right. Libby needed to date more. She had plenty of opportunities, but she always seemed to have more excuses.

Not anymore. Starting next week Libby McKay was in the market for Mr. Right. Or at the very least Mr. Right Now.

The next morning, Libby arrived bright and early at the Marchetti house bearing a carry-out tray full of iced cappuccino and a box of muffins from her mom's bakery. Sometime last night it had occurred to her that she had been less than supportive of Mel's new life plan. Now she was determined to make up for it. She found Mel, John, and Parker still taping up boxes. This didn't really surprise her. Mel might have put a lot of thought into moving, but she had clearly left all the packing for the last minute. No complaining though—Libby silently joined the effort.

They didn't work quickly. Every 90 or so seconds, Melanie felt the need to stop and play 'remember when'. Caught up in her friend's nostalgia, Libby usually joined in reliving the moments of their youth. These trips down memory lane provided no end of amusement for the guys. Before long Parker and John were sharing increasingly outrageous fictitious memories of their own.

"John do you remember that time you saved all those kittens from the burning barn?"

"That was nothing compared to the time you carried that old lady with a broken leg ten miles to the emergency room."

"Well it isn't as though I had much of a choice. I would have driven her, but if you remember, you had borrowed my car to go on that safari."

"A safari in New York?"

"Don't be ridiculous, Libster—the safari was in Canada; that was probably why I needed a car." John was grinning like a ten-year-old at the idea.

"Sure! If I remember correctly they were hunting the ever elusive Canadian unicorn."

"What makes a unicorn Canadian?" Mel stopped giggling long enough to interject.

Parker made a face. "They live in Canada."

"Yeah." John looked excited. "And they don't have that pansy spiral horn these American unicorns are sporting. Nope, they each have a great big moose antler in the middle of their heads." John opened one hand, planted his thumb in the center of his forehead and childishly galloped about the room a few times. The four friends erupted into laughter.

"Did you catch one?" Mel managed when she caught her breath.

"Of course he did!" Parker piped up. "And you know if you catch a unicorn they have grant you a wish."

"I thought that was leprechauns." Libby stood up and began to gather the remnants of their breakfast to take out to the trash.

"Nah, leprechauns aren't real," John answered with mock seriousness.

"What did you wish for?"

John didn't even stop to consider. "The Laker Girls."

Mel whirled around irritably to face him, knocking Libby backwards at the same time. The remnants of two now melted cappuccinos splashed across Libby's tee shirt. "Mel!" Libby pulled the wet and stained cotton away from her skin. "Tell me you have something in one of these boxes I can wear."

Giggling, Mel shook her head. "You know anything I own would look positively indecent on you." It was true. Libby's much more pronounced bust line had long ago put an end to any closet sharing.

"Maybe your mother?" But Libby knew that Mel had inherited her figure from Mrs. Marchetti and she was unsurprised to see Melanie shaking her head a little mournfully.

The coffees hadn't been *iced* for several hours now, but the liquid was still cold. That combined with her embarrassment caused her breasts to tighten and increase her embarrassment.

Ever the gentleman, Parker reached behind his back, grabbed a handful of cotton and dragged his own shirt over his head. "Here you go, Libby." He tossed it across the room to her and Libby retreated to the hallway bathroom to change and rinse the coffee out of her shirt. Parker was tall, and his shirt fell below the hem of her shorts. Cinching the material closer to her waist, Libby tugged the elastic band out her hair and used it to knot the excess material at the small of her back. When she returned to Mel's room, Parker was flexing his now bare muscles and taunting John for *letting himself go*. Libby stood for awhile in the doorway just watching her friends. Soon they would all be in New York and she would be in Tallahassee.

"Think you have enough clothes?" John laughed as he carried a heavy armload of garment bags over to a pile of suitcases. It had taken all morning and part of the early afternoon to get her completely packed up. Libby would have been sorry for volunteering, except she was remembering how much fun the four of them could have together.

"A girl likes to look her best, you know," Mel answered sweetly, and stood on her tiptoes to give him a peck on the cheek.

John swept her off her feet into a big bear hug. "Babe, you can have all the clothes you like, but you know you look your best in nothing at all." He gave her butt an exaggerated squeeze to make his point.

"Dude! A little propriety, if you please." Parker made a big show of averting his eyes. "Let's start taking some of this out to the truck, Libby." He handed her a small pile of boxes, and hefted a heavy suitcase into each of his own hands. "You're going to leave me alone with those two walking hormones for a ten hour car ride! Are you sure you don't want to ride back with us?"

"Sorry, I have my own packing to do. And I have plans this weekend anyway."

"With Brian?"

"What!" Libby dropped the boxes she was holding a little harder than she had planned and spun to face Parker. "I'm sorry, what?" she tried to ask again, more composedly.

Parker's eyebrows drew close together. "That's your guy's name, right? Mel mentioned him, but she isn't always good with names."

Libby's heart lurched when she remembered thinking something similar about her friend during the Stephanie/Effie conversation. In the end it hadn't really mattered what her name was, except perhaps that she had been able to forgive her Aunt Stephanie for having the bad luck of sharing a name with Tony's girlfriend. All that had mattered was that Tony had a girlfriend. And okay, they had only lasted one summer, but that was a lot longer than any of Libby's boyfriends had lasted. This wasn't saying much since Libby had never really had a boyfriend.

How pathetic, she reflected; 19 years old and never had a real boyfriend.

"Libby? These are kind of heavy. Could you..." Snapping out of it, Libby stepped aside so Parker could unload his arms into the back of the moving truck. "I didn't mean to bring you down. Mel mentioned you were seeing someone, and I just thought he might be helping you with your packing. If he isn't coming I could stay an extra day and help you." Libby's eyes darted to Parker's face. She had felt so bad about unintentionally leading him on her senior year. He must have realized what she was thinking. "Calm down. I am not making a pass at you. I just thought that if you have as much luggage as Mel..."

"J. Lo doesn't have as much luggage as Mel," Libby quipped. "Brian is in Florida, and I am mostly packed and ready to go—but thanks for the offer. Besides, how would you get back to New York?"

"I am beginning to think missing out on this road trip would be worth the price of flying commercial." Parker grinned. Parker had a nice grin. Actually, Libby mused as she followed him back up the stairs, Parker had a nice everything. Tall and slim, he escaped appearing awkward and lanky with confident graceful movements. He had the kind of muscle tone you might get from swimming or running. He could have been a dancer, she thought. Some male ballet dancers were straight, right? Who was that guy from Dirty Dancing? Libby was pretty sure he had been a real dancer. Yes, Parker was certainly nice to look at. It was a crying shame that she couldn't convince her heart to beat even a little faster when he walked in the room, or persuade her skin to tingle whenever she heard his voice. If it weren't for those little details, Parker would have been a perfect candidate for Mister Right.

Parker paused, grimacing, outside Mel's closed bedroom door. Libby was pretty sure they had left it open. He knocked. "You guys still in there?" No answer. "We should really finish loading the truck if we are still planning on leaving tonight."

There was a heavy thud. Worried, Libby rushed towards the door, but Parker pulled her back, making a shushing motion by placing a finger on his lips.

Sure enough, Libby began to hear heavy breaths and soft moans. "Eww." She took an involuntary step backwards, yanking her hand off of the door knob as if it she had been burned. "They wouldn't…" She blushed.

Parker pounded on the door with the palm of his hand a few times. "Dude! Come on!"

"Get lost, Park," John finally answered through the closed door.

"What do you suggest *we* do?"

"Parker, my friend, if I have to explain that to you then you are beyond my help. Now get lost— you are embarrassing my girlfriend."

"Come on, Libby. We might as well go find some lunch." Parker was shaking his head as he led her back downstairs. Libby was speechless.

In the kitchen, Libby pulled out all the ingredients for grilled cheese sandwiches and Parker manned the frying pan. "Should we make something for John and Mel?"

Parker wrinkled his face. "No way. Although I bet they're working up quite an appetite. They can make their own when they've… finished."

Libby found herself blushing again. "Parker, do you think we—I mean, John seemed to think we…" She wasn't actually sure how to ask her question. "Well, we almost before, and maybe now…"

Parker laughed. Loud, knee slapping, slightly obnoxious laughter.

"I didn't think it was that funny!" Libby was so mortified she barely remembered what just plain embarrassed felt like. "All I meant was... oh, never mind, it was dumb."

"I'm sorry, Libby. I shouldn't have laughed, but you looked so nervous and we didn't really *almost* anything." He slid a plate, with her grilled cheese on it, over the counter to her and took a big easy bite out of his.

"Last summer!"

"Sweetheart, if that's *almost* then—well, then I guess that explains your scarlet cheeks upstairs." He was laughing again.

"Oh, for Pete's sake!" Libby huffed. "I don't know why I bother."

Parker seemed to register the genuine distress on Libby's face. He walked around the kitchen island and spun her around to face him, bracing his arms on the counter on either side of her. "It would be awesome, Libby... for me. You are beautiful, and sexy, and I have totally thought about it. But it would just be sex. And you aren't a 'just sex' kinda girl. Do you really want to trash two years of friendship for an hour of fun?"

"An hour?"

This brought more chuckling from Parker, and he dropped a light kiss on her nose.

"Damn, I like you, Libby! I wouldn't risk your friendship—even for three hours!" He whispered that last part into her ear before shoving off from the counter and returning to his lunch.

"I am surrounded by men determined to save me from myself. Lucky me."

"Is this about Brian? You two not getting along?" Parker was eating his lunch again.

"No, Brian is fine… but we aren't really together. Just forget it, okay?" Libby stuffed her mouth full of grilled cheese to force herself to stop rambling.

Chapter Eight

Outside, Tony was pacing around the driveway. He had been so happy to be home a moment ago. But then he had walked in and seen Libby wearing what was obviously Parker's shirt, since Parker himself wasn't wearing one, and what Libby was wearing must have been five sizes too big. Tony wasn't really a violent guy, but it took all his self control not to rush in and pummel the guy when he had leaned in to kiss her. As soon as he had regained his motor functions, Tony had quietly backtracked to the front door.

Why hadn't he known that Parker and Libby were still together? Libby hadn't mentioned it, but then barring one late night inebriated phone call (which still haunted his dreams three months later) they had pretty much avoided all things romantic. It wasn't as if he thought she sat home alone every weekend, but there was a pretty big difference between knowing she was dating and having to witness it in his kitchen! Where the crap was he going to eat his breakfast cereal from now on? He sure as hell wasn't ever going to be able to sit at the kitchen counter again.

Okay, he had to get a handle on this. Tony concentrated on taking deep breaths. Libby hadn't spoken to him for five months after that party. After the night he had basically chased her into Parker's arms. He was so stupid! She had been right there and he had pushed her away. He had actually reminded her that Parker had been her date. Told her that *of course Parker wanted to be more than friends.* Stupid! No. He wasn't going to think about that. He was just going to remember that, during those long quiet months, he had sworn to himself that he wouldn't make any more dumb mistakes where she was concerned. And if that meant being just friends then that was what he would do, because he wasn't prepared to lose her again. Maybe he should just drive around town for awhile. How long until Mel was leaving for New York? Surely Parker would be leaving then too. When he came back he could take his friend Libby out to dinner, and maybe a movie, and maybe an ice cream after that.

Just as he had made up his mind and was heading for his car, he heard the front door open.

"Tony!" Turning, he saw Libby running towards him. "You're early," she said as she slipped her arms around him for a too-brief hug. "You weren't leaving, were you?" Libby glanced between him and his car.

Yes, he thought, I am leaving so I don't put your dumb shirtless boyfriend through a wall. What he said was, "Oh, no. I was just making sure I locked it."

"Well, come on. Mel is your sister; it is only fair that you help us carry some of her crap down to the truck." Libby towed Tony into the house.

Awkwardly, Tony joined everyone in the kitchen, where John and his sister were finishing lunch. "So... Did Mel make you guys do all the packing?"

"No."

"Yes."

"Yes."

"Yes."

Everyone spoke at once.

Tony smiled a little, but he couldn't keep from glaring at Parker. Finally catching on, Parker cleared his throat. "Oh, Libby is just borrowing my shirt until hers dries." Tony raised his eyebrows.

"Because she spilled coffee…" Parker trailed off, his usual confidence shaken.

"Well, I'm sure you'll want it back before you guys get on the road." Tony turned to Libby. "You can help yourself to anything in my bedroom. You know where that is." Libby looked a little confused but she headed off down the hall anyway. When she returned she had traded one oversized shirt for another and Tony barely restrained himself from pounding on his chest caveman style.

A couple hours later the truck was finally loaded, and they were saying their goodbyes.

"I don't think Mel's brother is my biggest fan." Parker smirked a little as he wrapped Libby in a one arm hug. The other arm was holding a barrel sized container of popcorn. Parker had proclaimed that he needed sustenance to deal with the upcoming road trip.

"Don't let it bother you. He is sometimes a bit overprotective of me." Libby pulled a face. "Like most big brothers."

"Right, but he isn't your big brother, is he?" Humor danced across Parker's face.

"Tell him that," Libby murmured into Parker's shoulder.

"I think he can work it out on his own." Parker put a friendly hand on Libby's cheek. "You okay? You've been a little off all day."

"End of summer blues, I guess. Remind Mel to text me when you get there."

"You got it." Parker kissed her cheek and then climbed into the truck. "See ya. Have a good semester." The truck pulled away, and her friends left.

Shaking her head, Libby started back to the house. She had to snap out of this. It wasn't like they had excluded her from their little New York club on purpose. And she loved Tallahassee. Mel was right. Libby needed to go out more. And that would be on the first order of business when she returned to school next week.

Tony watched Libby through the window. He had already made arrangements to meet John and Mel in the city for dinner at the end of the week. Having accepted a full time position at the *Examiner*, Tony would be in New Jersey. He would be able to see a lot more of Mel than Libby would, so he had left them alone to say goodbye. Also, he had reached his Parker tolerance level at least 45 minutes ago. And he was pretty sure Libby wouldn't appreciate it if he decked her boyfriend. Maybe he would get lucky and Parker would choke on a piece of popcorn.

The rest of the evening was more fun. Tony took Libby to a movie. The movie was bad, but it didn't matter because it was so bad it was funny. After the movie they got a pizza—half Hawaiian for Libby, and half pepperoni and sausage for Tony. They talked as they ate. Libby told Tony how she had fallen in love with St. George's Island, and about the sea shell collection she and Suzy had started. Tony talked about being full time at the paper, and how he had his own cubicle—well, his own desk with a shelf anyway. Tony was a little disappointed in being assigned to the sports section, but he was working on a few human interest pieces that one of the editors had said were 'not bad'. Libby complained mournfully about needing to take sophomore accounting, and about how her friend Brian wouldn't even be available for tutoring this year because he was doing a year abroad with his girlfriend.

"Maybe he can tutor you over the phone," Tony teased.

"Right—he's going to Australia. It's a 14 hour time difference! And I am so not paying that phone bill."

"14 hours! Wow. I mean, I knew it was far, but geez. Still though, it's probably pretty cool. You should tell him to check out the toilets—I hear they flush backwards."

Libby laughed. "I think that's an old wives' tale, but I will get him to find out for you. If I were going to do a year abroad—you know, if I hit the lottery—I think I would rather see Europe. Maybe Rome. Or Paris—the French are all about pastries!"

They kept talking until the pizza was cold. There was no use in leaving two slices though, so with exaggerated self sacrifice they each lifted a slice from the tray. "Fruit does not belong on a pizza," Tony declared as he picked an errant piece of pineapple off his slice and offered it to her disdainfully. Libby's hands were full with her own slice of pizza, and she reacted without thinking. Leaning in, she nibbled the fruit out of Tony's hand.

Desire, white hot, shot through Tony's nervous system. Her soft wet lips closed over the tips of his fingers. Her tongue flickered against pad of his thumb and her teeth scraped lightly against his skin. It only lasted half a second, but Tony was rooted speechlessly to his seat. Libby realized belatedly the intimacy of her actions, and she snapped back to her side of the table and began eating with great focus.

The tension was still thick between them when the waitress brought their check. Libby reached for her purse, but Tony waved her off with a flick of his hand.

"You forget, Lib. I'm gainfully employed these days." Tony's grin went a long way to ease Libby's nerves. "Not *very* gainfully, but I am happy to spring for dinner. Especially since the movie was my choice and it was basically a waste of two hours of your life."

"You paid for the movie too, so Skee Ball is on me." Libby pulled a few bills from her purse and skipped over to the coin machine in the small arcade area. Tony was glad to have a few minutes sitting alone while he waited for the waitress to return with his change. He needed the time to compose himself before he joined Libby in the arcade, or else he was going to be embarrassed. *4 times 6 is 24, 4 times 7 is 28, 4 times 8 is 32....*

By the end of the evening, Libby had thoroughly and humiliatingly trounced Tony's Skee Ball score and between them they had earned enough tickets for a bag of sour patch candies, a beaded bracelet, and a plastic sheriff's badge. Tony proudly pinned the badge to his shirt pocket as they walked down Main Street to where they had parked their cars behind the bakery.

"Hey, where's your bracelet?" he asked around a mouthful of the gummy candies.

Libby pulled it out of her pocket and waved it at him. "Right here."

Tony took the child's bracelet from her and snapped it free of the cardboard packaging. He was very solemn as he slid the bracelet over Libby's hand. Before he could dissuade himself he placed a soft open mouthed kiss to the inside of her wrist, imagining he could feel her pulse jump. Dropping their hands between them he wordlessly laced their fingers together and continued down Main Street as though the two of them walked hand-in-hand on a regular basis. Had he ever noticed how slim her wrists were before? Of course not. He had never noticed any woman's wrists before, because only Libby had the power to reduce him to a depraved-sex-obsessed-Neanderthal.

He had tried—to notice other women, that is. All year he had been determined to find someone. Anyone he could feel even a fraction of this connection with. It hadn't worked. He had found himself depositing his dates back their front doors at the end of each night with polite excuses of early classes or worries of onsetting colds, and he then he had gone home—alone.

"What do you want to do tomorrow?" Tony spoke as they reached their cars.

"Umm... I don't know. Don't you have to spend some time with your parents?" Libby thrilled at the idea of spending an entire day with him. But she didn't want to assume things, and then there were those old bad habits she needed to keep clear of. After all, hand holding and plastic bracelets did not undying devotion make.

"I think we should make cookies. You suck so far as a teacher, but I am willing to give you another shot." Tony disregarded her question.

"You want me to teach you how to bake?"

"Just how to bake cookies," He corrected her. "I have really missed your chocolate chip cookies. I could come to the bakery."

"Nah. You are a health code violation. We can go to my mom's apartment."

"Gee, you really know how to knock a guy down!"

Libby twitched a smile at him. "Don't take it personally. You have to pass a food safety course to use our kitchen."

"Okay, so tomorrow it is. Around 2:00?"

"2:00 is fine."

They had arrived at the bakery and were standing outside Libby's car, both unwilling to end the evening.

Tony weighed his options. He could hug her—pull her into his arms, fill his hands with her hips, smell her shampoo… Of course, kissing her goodnight would be better. A brief brush of his mouth against hers would be innocent enough, if less than satisfying. What he wanted to do was back her up against the car and devour her mouth. That mouth that he felt sure he could drown in, and still die happy. And her throat; he needed to know what her skin would taste like along her neck. He wanted to touch her, to feel the weight of her breasts, the softness of her skin… Okay, that option was out.

Instead of all of those things he raised their still intertwined fingers, dropped a kiss on the back of her hand, and said, "Night, Lib," before he walked back to his own car.

Chapter Nine

The next day Tony arrived as promised right at 2:00. Libby set out all the ingredients for chocolate chip cookies. It was the most fun Libby ever remembered having with Tony. And that was saying something because Libby always had fun with Tony. She found her mother's pink *Big or Small Save Them All* apron (left over from a breast cancer awareness bake sale a few years before). Of course, being the champ that he was, Tony donned the apron without comment. They worked most of the morning. Libby didn't often make one batch of cookies. That's what comes from growing up with a baker. So they ate the first batch while they made batches two through nine to be donated to the local lions' clubs for the annual apple festival the following week. Batch number ten Libby wrapped up for Tony to take back to New Jersey with him.

Under Libby's watchful eye Tony didn't burn a single tray of cookies, and he kept his tasting-spoon out of the raw dough. Even after spending the entire previous evening together, Libby and Tony found conversation flowed easily throughout the afternoon.

"Thanks, Lib. I won't tell you how quick those are going to get eaten, or how much extra time I am going to have to spend at the gym." Tony was doing the dishes, talking over his shoulder at her. There was something almost tender about that moment that kept Libby from replying. She was sure her voice would crack if she tried to speak. So many times in her greatest *when-I-grow-up* fantasies she had pictured similar situations. Only the dishes wouldn't have been left over from a baking lesson so much as left over from dinner. A roast she had spent all afternoon on for her, and Tony, and their three kids. Kids that would have had Tony's chocolate hair and Italian skin tone. But that was in the past. And hadn't Libby grown up since the days of waiting for Tony to see her as more than a friend? So she pushed those thoughts aside. There would be no roast, and no olive skinned babies.

It was almost dinner time. Tony dried his hands after stacking the last of the cookie sheets in a drying rack. He turned and watched where Libby was wiping down the counters. There was flour in her hair, and on her hands, and smudged up to her elbows. God, she was pretty. He wanted to walk up behind her and tell her that she made flour look good. He wanted to tug the braid out of her hair and let if fall through his fingers. There were a lot of things he wanted to do.

"Should we get some food? Or I know an arcade where I can let you win at Skee Ball again?" Tony wasn't hungry after an afternoon of cookies, but he didn't want to go home either.

"In your dreams, Marchetti." Libby hadn't eaten nearly as many cookies as Tony and she was starving, but she felt a distinct emotional backslide coming on, and needed time to get her head together. "I'm not really that hungry. And I have a lot of packing to do still. Rain check?"

Inside, Tony crashed. "Yeah, too many cookies—I'm sure I couldn't eat either." Carefully, he pulled out his cheeriest fake smile (the one usually reserved for Great Aunt Millicent, who smelled like cats, but who Dad insisted on inviting for Thanksgiving anyway) and started gathering his jacket to leave. "Tomorrow. What would you like to do tomorrow?"

He was trying to kill her. "I have to leave pretty early Monday morning and I am sure your parents want to spend time with you."

Even his Aunt Millie smile was failing him. But Tony was nothing if not determined. "Okay, well get your packing finished tonight. And I will pick you up in the morning. We'll go to the Y and run." Smooth, he thought to himself. She was going to dust him—so not the way to impress a girl. "And when we come back I will help you load your boxes so you'll be able to sleep in a little on Monday."

Accepting her defeat and unable to resist the idea of sharing her morning run with Tony, Libby nodded. "I like to get to the gym early."

Tony breathed a sigh of relief that she had agreed. "I'll be here early."

And he was. With coffee. Tony knocked on the door and was surprised when Ms. McKay answered. This was dumb because, of course, Ms. McKay lived here. But she usually worked strange hours since bakeries were open so early, and Tony hadn't actually hung out here that many times.

"Come in, Tony. Libby's changing; she should be out in a moment. Have a seat."

Tony thanked her and perched himself on the couch, sipping the still scalding coffee to cover for his nerves. He remembered very clearly the night Ms. McKay had come home in the early morning and found him and Libby fast asleep, wrapped up in each other on this very couch. When she had shaken Tony awake he had wanted to crawl under a rug. Although she had been very sweet about the whole thing. Thanking him for being such a good friend. For sacrificing his Halloween night and for tucking Libby back into her bed since the medicine had knocked her out cold. That had just made him feel worse, because of course Tony had had his own less than honorable reasons for being there that night.

"Libby tells me you're living in New Jersey?"

Oops, stop daydreaming man! Ms. McKay was talking. Had he missed something?

"Umm, yeah. I have been interning at a paper there the past few years. So it was an easy choice." He didn't mention that he had been researching papers in Tallahassee a little over a year ago. That was before the luau party, and before Parker.

"A newspaper man?" Ms. McKay smiled. He could see a little of Libby's smile in her face. He wondered if this was Libby twenty years from now. Libby must have gotten her height from the late Mr. McKay, but the shining dark eyes and flyaway dark curls were all there in her mother. "Would I have seen your writing?"

"Not unless you get the Columbia literary mag, or you unless read the obits in the Trenton *Examiner*." Tony offered a sheepish shrug. "The *Examiner* is a small paper, but I like that. I'm not sure I want to be *Perry White*; I am looking forward to being given more interesting subject material now that I have my degree."

"Hmm." She nodded politely. Maybe he should tell her he'd written a book, and that he had plans for more. No—that was still a bit of a pipe dream, not exactly promising of a secure future.

"The *Examiner* isn't a big paper, but it is well run. I've learned a lot. I think I might like to start my own paper one day. Taylorsville doesn't even have its own daily." Where did that come from? But it wasn't a bad idea, and Tony didn't want to live in New Jersey forever. He hadn't given much thought to moving since he gave up on the idea of Florida, but he found he liked the idea of moving home.

"That's nice, dear." Ms. McKay didn't seem impressed one way or another with his future plans. Not that his plans should matter to her. Parker was going to be a lawyer. Parker had the kind of bank account that could withstand monthly airline tickets just to take her daughter on a date or two. Stupid Parker.

Libby and Tony ran two one-mile legs. She smoked him both times. Silently Tony promised himself to hit treadmill more often at his own gym. Tony was no couch potato though, and when they settled into a light jog around the track he had less of a problem keeping up. Libby was beautiful when she ran. She was always beautiful, but there was calmness on her face when she was running. Relaxation vibes rolled off of her like she didn't have a care in the world. Not Tony—Tony's lungs were burning, and he could barely remember this morning's blueberry muffin. But Libby looked incredible. Of course, her amazing long legs in those tiny running shorts didn't hurt either.

"That was fun. I think I missed having someone to train with." Libby mopped her towel over her face and shoved it back into her bag. Tony would have answered if he had any breath to spare—which he did not.

After they had hit the showers Tony offered to help Libby load her things into the moving truck.

"I'm not picking up the U-Haul until tonight—it's cheaper that way."

"Oh, right."

"My mom and Stuart wanted to have lunch together."

"Oh, right. Well, I will get you home then."

Tony drove Libby back to her apartment in silence.

"Thanks for hanging out with me this weekend." Tony finally spoke when he stopped in front of her building. "Have a good drive tomorrow."

"Yeah. I've had fun. It was nice to have a friend around since Mel abandoned me early." Libby leaned over to hug him goodbye. Her hair, still wet from the shower at the gym, clung to his neck. Oh yeah, he thought, we are just friends.

Upstairs, Libby told herself she was thankful that Tony had left. She reminded herself of her resolution to move forward with her life. She did not sit around dwelling on how she had felt with Tony's eyes on her legs and bottom for the past hour. Well, not much.

Chapter Ten

It was easy falling back into school. Suzy was bubbling with how wonderful her summer had been, and how she had gotten back together with her high school boyfriend. Accounting wasn't quite as bad as she had remembered. And of course the Florida weather was a plus.

Keeping her resolution to move forward with her life, Libby set out to really enjoy college life. She accepted dates and went to parties. Not that she let her studies slide, but she didn't feel as if she was being left behind either. Not really.

Brian flushed a toilet—he says the water just dumps straight down. Something about the way the Australian toilets are shaped. Sorry to disappoint you.

-L-

I'm not disappointed. I bet he is just pulling your leg. I choose to stand strong in my backwards flushing toilet beliefs.

-t-

They are letting my take over Sarah Kendall's column while she is on maternity leave. This is a big deal.

Halloween at the office was great. I was Clark Kent.

-t-

Congrats! Send me copies!

I was a pirate wench—the accent was fun.

-L-

I haven't been home for Thanksgiving turkey in a while. I am pretty excited. When are you getting home?

-t-

Mom and Stuart are going away for Thanksgiving. I am glad; she doesn't take many vacations. I am going to New York to see Mel.

-l-

My mom got married!!! She came home from Thanksgiving married! They eloped in Las Vegas— so weird. I like Stuart and all—I just can't believe they did it in Vegas! It is too romantic for grownups.

-L-

Wow. Stuart's pretty cool. He was my little league coach, you know. I bet they are happy. I am sure it is weird for you.

I heard Mel scorched the turkey! Serves you right for abandoning me in Taylorsville. If you want to talk you can call me.

-T-

We missed you at Christmas, Lib. I wish you had mentioned that you were staying at school to take a winter class. I have a little vacation time coming up—I was thinking of spending it in Florida. What do you think?

-t-

"Hi, Tony."

Libby was sitting in her dorm room. She had picked up her phone as soon as she saw his name flashing on the caller ID.

"Libby! You will never guess. I mean, I had almost given up on sending it out—but I'm nothing if not persistent…"

"Tony! You are starting to remind me of Mel." Libby smiled into the phone. She had missed his voice. He was coming for a visit next week and Libby couldn't wait. She had a list as long as her arm of things she wanted to show him.

"Sorry, Lib." Tony drew a deep breath. "I got an agent."

"For your book? That's amazing. Wow. I told you it was good."

"I know. You have been really great. You are the only one I have told, you know. I'm still not telling anyone—not until I get a publisher. But an agent is a huge start. He is really optimistic, and he has already hooked me up with an editor in the city. I am going to meet with her next week."

"Next week?"

"I know, Lib. That's one of the reasons I am calling. I have to cancel my trip. I don't want to, but I only get so much vacation time. And I think it would be better spent working with my editor. *My editor*, can you believe it?"

"Of course it's fine. Great, actually. I am super happy for you." Stupid book! Her whole week was ruined. Except it wasn't a stupid book. It was very good and Tony was a great writer.

"I knew you'd understand. Libby—I don't deserve friends like you. Mr. Carson, Jack, he's the agent. I sent him a bunch of sample stuff in addition to the manuscript and he likes it all. He agrees with me about Isaac Raines being the strongest character. I am already outlining a few stories. I told you about Isaac, right?"

"Umm, no."

"He's a detective. A real wrong-place-wrong-time kind of a guy. Think John McClain, only less pissy."

"John McClain is not pissy!" Libby loved the Die Hard movies.

"Missing the point here, Lib." Tony was laughing at her.

"Oh right. Sorry. Okay, tell me all about your editor and about your new book."

They talked late into the night. Tony was so excited. And he should be. This was a huge deal, but still Libby felt sad. She hated feeling jealous. But she had to admit, if only to herself, that she was actually very jealous. Of a book. Well, not really of the book—it just seemed like she was stuck in a holding pattern. All around her people were doing things, making futures. And she was just happy to get a passing grade in accounting.

Mel had just signed a deal with a boutique in SoHo (because when you live in New York you do things like go to boutiques in SoHo). She was going to be offering Marchetti Designs in women's dress shops. Apparently women are the ones buying men's accessories anyway. John and Parker were looking at medical and law schools. Suzy spent most of her nights at her boyfriend's apartment these days and was beginning to hint at an engagement. Even boring Brian and his boring girlfriend were having the time of their lives in Australia. Dependable old Libby was just plodding along towards a business degree.

Tmarchetti: You there?

Libby thrilled at the ping of the chat window on her computer screen.

Libbylibbylibby: I was just finishing a paper. Yeah, I'm here.

Tmarchetti: I had a meeting with my agent in the city today. I ate dinner at Mel's. Have you talked to her lately?

Libbylibbylibby: Not in a couple of weeks actually. She's so busy. Is everything okay with her?

Tmarchetti: She's fine. Can I call you?

Libbylibbylibby: Of course.

"Hello?" Libby was starting to get worried. She should have called Mel to catch up. But school had been crazy lately.

"Hey. Lib." Tony sounded strange.

"What's going on?"

"So I was in the city today. And I was at Mel, and John's place. And Parker stopped by."

"Okay. What's going on Tony?"

"Libby, he had a girl with him. And I didn't know if you knew or what the deal was, but you should know. And you are a thousand times prettier—if that helps. I can't imagine what he's thinking."

"Tony! Are you trying to warn me that Parker has a new girlfriend? Her name is Penny. I've met her. I like her." Geez! She'd really been worried and here it was just his overprotective brother routine.

"So you two aren't together anymore?"

"No. We never were. Not really. Just a few dates and a great friendship. Seriously, my heart is intact. But thanks for worrying about me. That was sweet."

"You weren't *together*?" Anger laced through Tony's voice. "That's not what it looked like when you were sharing a wardrobe with him last summer!"

"At the risk of repeating myself—Parker and I are just friends." Libby tired to keep her voice even. This was none of his business.

"So you were what? Friends with benefits? A way to pass time when he was in town? I should kill him."

Now that kind of pissed Libby off. "No, you shouldn't do anything, Tony! Because you aren't responsible for me; you aren't *my* big brother. Even if you were, I am an adult and old enough to know which and what type of friends I want in my life."

"I know how old you are, Lib," Tony ground out. "Sorry. I just—I don't want to see you hurt, Libby." It sounded like he was calming down.

"Parker has never hurt me."

Tony winced. He knew he had been the one to hurt Libby, but things were different now. "So Parker has Penny and you…?"

"And I am happy for them."

"Okay. When are you finished classes?"

Libby was relieved that Tony had changed the subject. She really didn't want to have to discuss her relationships with Tony. She gave him the dates of her final exams (which were still several weeks away) and when she expected to return to North Carolina. They talked for awhile about how it would be strange for her to be going 'home' to Stuart's town house instead of the building where she had grown up. And when Tony could hear her yawns through the phone line, he sent her to bed.

Chapter Eleven

Tony was waiting for her when she got to the bakery the morning after she returned to Taylorsville. He was leaning against the back door with his arms crossed over his chest and a mile-wide grin split across face. This was a new smile. Not quite her coveted only-for-Libby smile. Somehow it was more challenging, and a little predatory, but that had to be her sleep deprived mind playing tricks on her.

He lifted her into a long tight hug. "I missed you, Lib." His soft whisper fell into her hair just above her ear, and Libby felt a thrill she hadn't allowed herself to indulge in since high school.

"What a surprise." She managed to speak when he had set her back down and she was able to get the key into the door.

Tony followed her inside and watched her silently as she began preheating ovens and getting ready for the business day. It took all his self control not to kiss her senseless. It was only 5:00 in the morning. Her hair was pulled tightly into a ponytail and there wasn't a trace of makeup on her face. She was the most beautiful thing he had ever seen. But he wanted to be cautious. No more assumptions or misunderstandings. Tony was going to get this right and that meant keeping his libido in check for awhile longer.

"Okay, are you going to tell me what you're doing here?" Libby broke the silence.

"I told you—I missed you." Tony flashed her his most charming smile.

"At 5:00 in the morning?"

"Especially at 5:00 in the morning." His smile grew a little suggestive. "I'm in town for a couple of days. I would have been at Stuart's yesterday, but I thought your mom might want you to herself."

"Actually, Mom and Stuart did have a big dinner waiting when I got there. They had some pretty amazing news, too."

"I have some amazing news myself." They had moved into the dining area, and Tony wordlessly joined her in lowering chairs off tables onto the floor. "Well, some of it is news, and I have something else I want to talk to you about."

"What's that?"

"Well, first… Jack sold *Thrills*! It is a small run, but they are talking a multi-book contract based on some sample chapters from the Isaac Raines books. It is a big deal…" Tony didn't get to finish talking because Libby rushed him, throwing her arms around in a warm uninhibited hug.

For a second Libby was embarrassed at her actions, but Tony's arms circled her waist without hesitation. He crushed her body to his and lifted his big hands to frame her face. His mouth took hers in a passionate hungry kiss. Rough skinned fingers trailed down her neck. His hands opened and skimmed down her back. Heat from his skin burned a path down her spine through her thin tee shirt. When she felt the tips of his thumbs brush the underside of her breasts, she gasped. Tony growled into her kiss; his tongue explored her mouth with abandon. Gripping her waist, he easily lifted her onto a stool. Instinctively, Libby parted her knees, inviting him closer. He stepped into her, gliding his hands down past the hem of her shorts and massaging the bare skin of her exposed thighs. Lifting one of her legs to wrap around him, Tony ground his hips into her.

Heat pooled in Libby's midsection. She could clearly feel Tony's arousal even through the material of their clothing. Drunk with the power she had over him, she scraped her nails lightly down his back, and when she reached the waist band of his jeans she urged him to press harder and closer. Slipping her hands under the hem of his shirt, she gave herself access to all of his heavenly hard muscles. She mapped him with her palms as she pressed hot open mouth kisses down his neck until she was nibbling his collar bone.

"Ungh, Libby!" Tony rasped. He had one hand buried in her hair, the twister long since tugged loose and discarded, and the other wrapped around her knee, holding her tight to him. Libby had never known how wonderfully erotic a touch to the back of her knee could be. "We have to stop," he managed through his panting breaths.

"No way." Libby nipped at the skin on his neck, and lifted her face for another taste of his lips.

"Stop." Tony wrenched his hands from her beautiful soft smooth skin. He gripped the counter behind her, caging her in his arms but no longer touching her.

Libby felt a cold rush over her at the loss of his skin against hers. "Right, just friends." Libby looked everywhere but into his eyes.

"No, sweetheart." Tony's voice was husky and tender between panting breaths. "I just didn't mean for that to happen." He chuckled lightly. "You do have a history of messing with my plans. You know?" Libby looked confused. "There is a wall of windows behind me. I was this close to taking you right on that stool," Tony whispered into the curve her neck between dropping kisses there.

"Okay, let's go in the back."

"I'm tempted, sweetheart, but that isn't how this should happen. Hard and fast between your mother's ovens? That isn't you."

Libby thought it probably could be her.

"We have a bad record with communication, you and me. We should talk first."

Oh. It was a little clearer now. Briefly she regretted allowing him to believe that she and Parker had had a sexual friendship. He was making sure she didn't have any expectations. That was fair, she thought, since he lived 1100 miles away from her. Fair didn't make it hurt any less. "Okay. Talk."

Tony pushed off of the counter and rocked back on his heels. He ran a hand over his face and through his hair. Libby loved when he did that. "Just give me a moment to reboot my brain. I don't want to get this wrong—communication problems, remember?" A smile played at the corner of his mouth. "Talk to me, Libby. Distract me."

"Okay." Libby slid off her stool and smoothed her clothes back into place. "Well. My bedroom in Stuart's house is the size of a postage stamp. He says he is going to switch it with his home office, but he hasn't gotten around to it. There is barely enough room for my bed."

"Libby!" Tony's eyes were dark with heat, but he balanced his expression with a laughing smile. "About something other than a bed, please."

"Oh." Color flushed her cheeks. She busied herself loading the display cases with fresh muffins. "Well, Mom and Stuart did have some pretty great news. They are sending me to Rome."

"What? You're going to Italy? Like a summer vacation?"

"No, for school. They are paying for year abroad. I guess Stuart feels bad about excluding me, uprooting me…" A rolling motion with one arm showed that he had many reason and she wasn't really concerned with what they were. "So I am going to Rome."

"For a year? You are leaving for—a year." Tony was floored. Here he had been about to lay out his heart to her. Declare his intentions, so to speak. And she was leaving. He was nothing more to her than Parker had been. When had he ever thought he would be feeling bad for Parker? But now he was. She had cast him aside just as she would be doing to Tony at the end of the summer… when she left the country.

His silence seemed to encourage her, so she kept talking as she unlocked the front doors and finished her morning routine. "I told him it wasn't necessary, but he was determined. And I really want to go, so I gave in pretty easy. There is a cooking school an hour or so away from the college with a great pastry program, and I could be learning from the best about biscotti, budino, and tiramisu, and all while I work on my business degree. I think I really needed to do something like this. I mean, you have your writing, and Mel has her designs, and Parker's forever going on about law school choices…"

"I don't want to talk about Parker!" Tony was angry

"O—kay…" Libby drew out the word thoughtfully. This was ridiculous. Here she was blabbering on, waiting for him to screw up the courage to ask for no-strings sex? No way. "Listen, we're good, Tony. This was probably a bad idea. We aren't *that* kind of friends, right? We just got caught up in the moment. Forget about it."

"Of course. You're right, Lib. I gotta go, okay? I'll talk to you tomorrow, 'kay?" Tony strode quickly out the front door, and when he got to his car he pulled out his cell phone and called the Tallahassee News Journal to cancel his job interview.

Tony was gone 20 minutes before Libby realized that he hadn't gotten around to telling her his 'something else'.

Chapter Twelve

"Oh my God! I can't believe you are leaving!" Mel gushed at the airport. Just like she had gushed in the car on the way to the airport, and like she had gushed on the phone when Libby had tried to tell her it was silly for her to come all the way home just to ride to the airport.

"We can talk all the time, Mel—the marvel of modern technology."

"It won't be the same!"

"Okay, babe—give her a hug and let her get through security. We don't want her to miss her flight." John tried to calm Mel down. Silly John. Mel lived for this stuff. "Have a good flight, Libster; call us when you get settled."

"Oh! I almost forgot! Tony said to wish you good trip too."

That got her attention. Libby hadn't seen Tony since the day of the bakery incident.

Apparently he had gotten a call that afternoon to go to a meeting with some people from his publisher about the Isaac Raines books and had left that night. They had talked, of course, and emailed. But things felt weird between them. They both determinedly avoided discussing the kiss in the bakery, but Libby guessed it would take some time before the weirdness could dissipate. She was glad anyway—she was willing to accept that Tony was okay with casual sex. That was fine, but she would be damned if she was going to be his *warm and willing body*. All week, all summer really, after the kiss at the bakery Libby's brain had battled with her hormones. At the time she had wanted him more than she had wanted her next breath, but she only needed to remind herself of Mel's graduation party, when he had explained about not being able to help how his body reacted. Explained to her that his only reactions to her were physical. That hurt she had felt at being nothing more than an itch to scratch had lasted months and she wasn't willing to go through it again.

"Tell him thanks for me, and I'll call him… you know, after I call you."

Mel snorted. "Yeah sure, right *after* you talk to me. Listen, Lib, do yourself a favor. Find some hot Italian guy and work my idiot brother out of your system. Have a hot and steamy European adventure."

"I am not going to Europe to have a fling!"

"Well, you should be. I know all that higher education will take up a lot of time, but surely you can spare a few nights over the next year. Think about it—they will all have accents!"

"Okay, I will think about it." Libby had no intention of doing any such thinking, but this was the best way to deal with her best friend when pressed for time.

Libby and Mel hugged tightly. And Libby set off with the mob of people headed for metal detectors.

Glad things are going well. You should mail me some Italian style chocolate chip cookies!

Only 5 weeks left until Thrills *is released. I am so stoked. You won't be able to buy it in Italy, but I will mail you a copy.*

-t-

I preordered my English copies on Amazon last month! But maybe you could mail me one anyway—signed. And when I am old I can sell my first edition signed Marchetti for eight million dollars.

Rome is beautiful. The school arranged for a lot of tours when we first got here, but now that I am making friends I am seeing all the local *stuff too.*

-L-

Dear Libby,

I never know what to say in these things! Miss you, Lib! So does John. How is the Italian man hunt coming?

Love, Mel

Dear Mel,

So far the well is still dry.

Love, Libby

When Libby got Tony's package in the mail, she tore it open right in the elevator of her building. She couldn't wait. Inside she found two copies of *Thrills, by the up and coming author Anthony Marchetti.* When she opened the first book she found

Tony's familiar but messy handwriting inside the cover.

Thanks for never doubting me!

Love, Anthony Marchetti

I just got your package! The book is perfect! Not that I thought it wouldn't be, but it is. I passed a copy (not the one you signed; that I am saving to fund my retirement) around my friends. One girl complained she wouldn't sleep for a month. High praise.

-l-

Ps: Is it weird that I want to tell you I'm proud of you?

She didn't go home for Christmas. She went skiing with a group from the university. She missed her family, and her friends. But she loved Rome and her new friends. A feeling deep in her bones told her that she needed this time. She needed her European adventure even if wasn't going to be hot and steamy.

Dear Libby,

I'm glad skiing was great. And thanks for the bolt of Italian leather! I can't tell you how excited my distributer is about Italian leather belts and wallets.

Merry Christmas, Mel

Dear Mel,

Here it is just leather! Glad you liked it.

Love, Libby

I signed the deal today on Isaac Raines. And they are ordering a second run of Thrills.

I am thinking of relocating. What would you think of me moving back to Taylorsville?

-t-

Dear Libby,

I can't wait for you to come home. How is the fling coming—any prospects?

I don't think it is serious, but Tony brought a girl to Easter dinner. Just so you know.

Love, Mel

Libby didn't cry. She wanted to, but the urge to sob wasn't as strong as she thought it should have been. So instead of crying she went to a party. Conjuring Mel's fashion advice from her memory, Libby dressed with purpose. Her red dress molded to her body until it flared at her waist. Spinning in front of her mirror, Libby admired the way the material moved with her body and lifted teasingly with a wiggle of her hips. Strappy black heals and a full-on makeup application completed her look.

Lena, an Italian friend of Libby's from the culinary institute, had invited her to the party. Originally she had declined, thinking she would be out of place as the only tourist there, but staying home with her textbooks wasn't a good idea. In the cab, on her way to the club, Libby had second, third, and fourth thoughts. A part of her was afraid that when the shock of Mel's news wore off depression would settle in. Of all the ways that evening could end, a teary public meltdown was Libby's least favorite scenario.

Less than a year in Italy had given her enough Italian to order a meal, go shopping, and ask for a restroom. That was not enough to survive an evening at a local party. It was likely that most of these dancing, drinking, laughing people spoke better English than Libby, but she loathed being the ignorant American.

Lena introduced her around, but soon Libby found herself sitting at the bar sipping her wine and wondering if she could politely call herself a cab. She had come to the conclusion that having a fling was better in theory than in practice.

"Ballare?"

Libby turned to find a man, tall, dark and gorgeous enough to satisfy Mel's fling requirements. He was probably too old to be a student. Although there was a wide range of ages attending the culinary institute, so she couldn't be sure. His dress shirt was rolled up past his elbows and unbuttoned at the collar in deference to the heat of the room. A spray of chest hair showed through the opening of his shirt. And that solved an age old debate between Libby and Mel: chest hair or no chest hair. Chest hair was unquestionably sexy.

He cocked his head, waiting for an answer. "American?"

"Si. Yes I am, sorry."

He seemed to find that funny. "You are sorry that you are American?"

"No. I am sorry that I didn't understand what you said. I am still learning."

"I asked you to dance with me."

"Oh! Umm, sure... yes. Thank you."

He thought that was funny too. Standing up, they walked closer to the other dancers. Tall, this man towered over her even in her dancing shoes. Despite being dressed in a relatively loose button-up shirt, she could tell he was muscular. Big solid forearms bulged below his rolled sleeves, and his shoulder was hard beneath her hand. He was a wonderful dancer. This was lucky for Libby as she was not—and two poor dancers together are always a disaster. They danced for two or three songs, and he held her close enough to smell his cologne the whole time.

"Would you care to take a walk with me? Mia Bellezza?" He had to lean down and speak directly in her ear, because the music was much louder on the dance floor. Hot breath tickled her neck.

Libby stiffened. He clearly read the discomfort in her expression because he added, "It is too warm in here, and we cannot talk. We will go just outside. The street is well lit, and popular. I won't do anything to make you uncomfortable."

So Prince Charming is also a gentleman, she thought, and allowed herself to be led outside.

"What did you call me?" Libby asked when the quiet of street made conversation possible.

"Mia Bellezza."

Libby thought for a moment. "My pretty?"

"It sounds nicer in Italian, but yes. And you are quite pretty." He was smiling widely now, and he covered the fingers she had tucked under his arm with his free hand. They settled on a bench under a street light, just a little way from the entrance to the club.

"Does that make you the wicked witch of the west?" Libby laughed at the mental picture of this very masculine man in green face paint.

"Scusi?" He frowned.

"Like from *The Wizard of Oz*—in the movie the witch says, 'I'll get you, my pretty, and your little dog too!'"

Everything she said seemed to be funny to this man. He laughed loudly. "I can't say I have ever seen that movie." Touching her face briefly, he continued, "You make me laugh. Perhaps I should call you Mia Risata? I would rather call you by your name."

"Libby—it's short for Elizabeth." Duh, like he really need that clarification. Why was she so nervous?

"Elisabetta." His eyes crinkled like he was still laughing at her. "You see, everything sounds nicer in Italian, Betta."

"Oh." He was right; her name was much prettier in Italian. "Umm, what's your name?"

"Gio. It is short for Giovanni." He was teasing her! Libby laughed and the tension broke.

It was very late when Gio and Libby shared a cab, and he let her out in front of her building. Consumed by each other's company, they had barely noticed the hour. Gio wasn't a student. As a matter of fact he was a teacher at the culinary institute. Not for the pastry classes, and Libby was glad because that would have been awkward. He was 30 years old and the difference in their ages hadn't even fazed him. In addition to teaching classes Gio also owned a bistro. And this led to talking about her mother's bakery/café and Libby's own aspirations.

They talked about her program at the university, and he was impressed that she was keeping up with two sets of courses. And they discussed what sightseeing she had managed since arriving in Rome. Another round of laughter followed when she lamented that she hadn't had a motorbike tour.

"Like Audrey Hepburn!" he exclaimed.

"I'm not sure… did she ride a motorbike?"

This elicited more laughter. Gio laughed a lot. Libby hadn't decided yet if she was insulted or not.

"In Roman Holiday… it is very famous. You must see it."

And that was how they spent the evening: getting to know each other. Libby allowed herself only a small moment of comparison, and reflected that this was an experience she was missing with Tony. Because they would never have a need to stay up all night exploring each other's lives and personalities. When the cab stopped in front of her building, Gio had smoothly waved away her attempt to pay and he instructed the driver to wait until she was inside the building.

The next day, Libby slept in; she hadn't gotten into bed until almost sunrise, after all. Just before lunch time, Libby's door buzzed. "Betta, may I come up?" Gio's rich voice sounded through the intercom.

Glancing around her small room, Libby took in the mess. A pile of discarded clothing choices was still on the floor in front of her closet, left from dressing for the previous night. Her bed was still unmade, because of course she had only just climbed out of it. Gio will not be impressed, Libby, she scolded herself.

"I will come down," she answered. As quickly as she could move, Libby pulled on fresh clothes and brushed her hair back into a ponytail. No time for makeup; Libby settled for lip gloss applied in the elevator. Outside she found Gio leaned against a motorbike parked at the curb.

"Your chariot." Gio stepped towards her, gesturing behind him to the bike.

"You have a motorbike!"

"It is rented, actually. But the result is the same. Come for a ride with me."

And she did. They toured all the major sites. Most of which she had already seen, but she appreciated them differently in Gio's company. Their tour ended at the Trevi Fountain. Gio's large frame had no trouble parting through the tourists as he brought Libby close to the famous landmark.

"They say if you throw a coin into the fountain, you are sure to return to Rome one day."

Gio reached into his pocket and offered her a handful of coins. Libby knew the legend and she had in fact tossed a euro into the fountain her first week in Italy. Unwilling to break the magic of the afternoon with that confession, Libby chose a coin from Gio's palm, tossed it high into the air, and watched it splash into the water. Without tearing his eyes from Libby's face, Gio extended his arm and rotated his wrist. The remaining coins plunked into the fountain. "So that you might return many times, Mia Betta," he said when she raised her eyebrows at him.

Dear Mel,

I met someone! His name is Gio, and he incredible. He took me for a motorbike ride last week, and then he cooked me dinner a few nights ago. Next weekend he wants to take me up the Almalfi coast for a picnic on the beach at Positano.

Love, Libby

Ps: You would approve of his accent

Dear Libby,

Details!

Love, Mel

***

I hope things are well—you haven't written in awhile. I guess you are busy. I have to admit, the time has passed more quickly than I thought it would. I can't wait to see you this summer.

-t-

Sorry. I have been busy. The thing is, I won't be home this summer after all. I was accepted into a certificate program at the culinary institute. I am going to finish my degree at the American University of Rome *this fall, and then I will spend an eighteen-week term full time at the culinary institute. I could hardly believe my mother agreed to it, but it is an incredible opportunity.*

I can't wait for the first Raines book. I have all my friends pre-ordering copies. You'll be releasing in Europe before you know it!

-l-

That's great, Lib. I am happy for you.

-t-

Dear Libby,

We are getting married! I hope I looked surprised when John asked, but to be honest I found the ring weeks ago. We are planning for June—you'll be home by then, right? We have to have time for your maid of honor dress fittings.

Love, the future Mrs. Jonathan Evans

Dear Mel,

Congrats! Of course I'll be home. I should be back by the end of April, which leaves me plenty of time to plan a bachelorette party. I am so happy for you. John too.

Love, Libby

Can you believe it about Mel? I guess John has grown on me by now. But she seems too young to get married. Wow.

I left the Examiner. *I am renting an office in Taylorsville with an apartment above it. I have decided to start my own paper. What do you think?*

-t-

That's awesome, Tony! I want you to send me every issue!

-l-

Libby decided not to mention that Mel was an adult. It was probably time to let that old argument die.

***

I can hardly believe I am finished. The last few months were killer, but totally worth it. Why didn't you tell me that graduating college was such an affirming experience? It was sad not to have Mel and John here. But my mom and Stuart are staying in Rome for a second honeymoon and it has been good to see them. I know you're busy, but I wish you could have been here.

-l-

Chapter Thirteen

Affirming? Tony didn't remember his graduation feeling quite so profound. But he supposed it might be a girl thing. He probably could have gone, but he didn't think he could face Libby's Italian boyfriend.   Anyway, she would be home in a few months. Mel seemed sure that Libby was serious about this guy. But Libby was still planning on coming home, so that was as good as a green light for Tony. He knew he had handled her news badly before she left, but now he had had time to think about it and Libby had been right. She needed to go to Italy, and after all this time waiting an extra 20 months didn't seem like such a hardship. Moving on hadn't worked. Libby was burned so clearly into his brain that eventually Tony had given up taking other girls out.

Mel had been very clear in her verbal abuse of him when Libby had left for Italy. Apparently Libby deserved better than a few emails and phone calls. Apparently he had deprived Libby of 'flowers, and nights out, and all the things real couples did.' She was right: Libby did deserve those things. So when she came home, Tony would be ready. He had a new business, and he was house hunting now that the paper was supporting itself. He was a multi-published author. Which wasn't a lawyer or an Italian chef, but it certainly seemed to impress Libby. He would take her on real dates, and bring her flowers, and make her fall in love with him. This was clearly Tony's only option, since he was more certain now than ever that Libby was the only one for him.

Gio and Libby were sharing a late dinner at his bistro on Libby's last free day before her program at the culinary institute started. They had spent most of their free time together over the last few months. At first Gio had impressed Libby by not pressing her physically—sharing a few passionate kisses here and there but nothing more. Now she was getting impatient.

"Thank you for celebrating so much with me this week." Libby moved closer to him in the booth they shared.

"Prego, Mia Betta." Gio kissed her. There wasn't the all consuming heat she had felt in Tony's arms. But there was warmth, a slow comfortable burn.

"Maybe we could keep celebrating?" Libby winced at her own words. She sounded so corny!

"Ahh, Betta. I think that would be inadvisable." Gio tucked her under his arm.

"Am I a bad kisser?" Libby was shocked into asking a question that had been plaguing her for years. And she was, for once, relieved when Gio burst into laughter.

"Oh, Mia Risata!" Gio covered her mouth with a slow deliberate kiss. "You are quite skilled, I think."

"Then I must smell bad?" Libby covered her embarrassment with a joke.

"I am afraid there is someone else in your heart, no?"

"No." Libby wanted to be with Gio, she was sure of it.

"You will be leaving in a few months. I do not wish to make love to you knowing you are leaving."

"Oh." He had a point. She was leaving. And as much as she loved Rome, she knew she didn't want to live here permanently. She missed her friends and her family desperately.

"I have never been to America. Perhaps when you are finished your course and you have returned home—perhaps I could visit you? You can take me for a motor bike tour! And then we shall see, Betta."

Libby nodded.

Chapter Fourteen

Could America have a scent? Libby was sure she smelled 'home' when she stepped off the airplane. Mel and John were waiting for her, and she ran into a squealing jumping hug with her best friend. It was good to be home.

"Tell me you brought gifts!" Mel joked as she linked arms with Libby and left John to grab her bags.

The three of them drove back to Taylorsville in a blur of conversation bouncing so quickly between Italy and wedding plans that John wisely kept to himself.

Libby felt wonderful being home. She was even glad to see her postage stamp bedroom in Stuart's house. It was impossible for Libby to think of his townhouse as her home. She liked Stuart and she was glad he made her mom so happy, but it wasn't home. Of course, she was only going to stay there temporarily. She had a plan.

She was going to operate a catering/made to order business out of her mother's kitchen. First order: Mel's wedding cake. The idea was to build up a name, and save some money until she qualified for a business loan to open her own place. Stuart's house would do until she had at least found a location, because she wasn't quite sure that Taylorsville could accommodate two bakery cafes. Libby was resigned to relocating to another town.

On her second day home, after eating a slightly awkward but mostly enjoyable breakfast with Stuart (her mother having already left for work), Libby headed out the door for a run. She would have to make time to go and renew the membership at the Y, but in the meantime she didn't want to get out of shape. Walking out the door, Libby had just begun her stretches when she looked up to see Tony striding towards her.

Memories did not to justice to those beautiful legs. Nerves engulfed Tony, momentarily leaving him frozen on the sidewalk.

"Hi!" Libby bounded over to him for a hug.

Still immobilized, Tony barely managed to return her hug before she pulled away. "Hi." Smooth, Marchetti, Tony chided himself. "Got a minute?"

"Can you keep up?" Libby smirked at him playfully.

He wasn't dressed for a run, but he keenly remembered his last disgraceful attempt of keeping up with Libby, and he had been training, so he agreed. They kept their pace slow and steady, which Tony was grateful for in light of his heavy cargo shorts.

"So, are you settling back in?"

"Yeah, all 24 hours I've been home."

Tony winced a little. He had meant to give her more time. It was probably going to be hard for her to readjust. And then there was the matter of her needing to get over the Italian boyfriend. Tony hadn't been able to help himself; a need to see her had overwhelmed him. Well, seeing didn't satisfy all his needs, but it would do for now.

"Good. I know you are probably busy with, umm, settling in, but I thought you might like to go to the wine festival with me on Saturday?"

"The wine festival? You don't strike me as a wine guy."

"Well, I'm not." Damn it, this was crumbling fast. Mel had said Libby was really into wine these days. "But I am covering it for paper, and Mel says you know a lot about wine, so…."

"Yeah, okay. Sounds fun." Libby was panting a little. Tony felt a surge of pride that he hadn't been winded yet.

"Great. I'll pick you at 4:00?"

"How about I meet you at your office? I'd love to see it. I was hoping to talk with you anyway, about some ad space."

"Yeah, sure, that's fine. Come a little early; we can get you set up with whatever you need." Tony would have rather picked her up. But he could adjust.

They had circled the block several times by now, and Tony slowed to a walk.

"Had enough?" Libby taunted lightly as she jogged in place.

"Nah. I just have to get going. I am going to have to go back home and change now before I get to the office."

Libby's face dropped in remorse. "I'm sorry! I wasn't thinking! You should have just said!"

"Calm down, Lib. I'm the boss. I can be late if I want to… and today I wanted to. I'll see you, okay?"

"Okay."

Tony turned and walked to his car. Waving again out the window, Tony drove away.

Saturday came quickly for Libby. She had spent the early part of the week refining her business plan, and working out what sort of and what size ad she would want to run in the paper. She had a menu she wanted to include in the Sunday inserts, but she thought a daily ad would be beneficial too until she got a name built up. Tony's paper had become very popular and most of the town seemed to subscribe to *The Taylorsville Daily Press*.

Libby walked into Tony's office a little after 3:00.

"You're early." Tony popped his head out of a back office. "Just let me change my clothes." Tony disappeared back behind the door, and Libby concentrated on not thinking about him changing clothes.

The outer office was pretty small, but Libby supposed that a newspaper wasn't the sort of place that received a lot of foot traffic so that probably wasn't a problem. Across one wall there were a few coin operated newspaper dispensers, and what looked to be a photo printing kiosk. Looking to her left there was a reception desk, and behind that there were two smaller desks. One long wall was decorated with a mural that depicted an old fashioned busy newsroom. It was comic book style with curved lines indicating ringing phones, faceless reporters in suits and hats scurrying about, and a shouting red faced man that Libby suspected was supposed to be Tony. It was positively charming, and exactly something Libby would expect from Tony.

"I like it too."

Libby whirled around to face Tony. He had changed into a green collared shirt. Green was most definitely Tony's color.

"A couple of students from the high school did it for their senior project. Then we ran a story about the importance of arts in school curriculums." Tony guided her back towards his office. "The best part? All the drywall underneath that mural is chipped and cracked!" He cocked her a grin. "You can't tell a bit now—pretty smart, huh?"

"I would expect nothing less." Libby grinned back. "This place is great, Tony. Really great." Inside his office, Libby was unsurprised to find his desk strewn messily with papers. He never had been exactly neat. Hanging on the wall were three shadow box frames—one each for the first copy of the *Daily Press* and both his novels to date. In one corner sat a wire wastepaper basket, and the floor surrounding it was littered with crumpled paper balls. An image of how they got there sprung into her mind—typically Tony.

"Well, it barely supports itself, but it is more a work of love than anything else. I have a couple of teenagers willing to work part time for peanuts and bylines, and I am subletting the apartment upstairs now that I've moved out—that helps."

"Where did you move to?"

Pride and excitement colored Tony's face. "I bought a house. About two months ago. It's an old Victorian on Pine Street. The down payment took what was left of my book advance, I can't afford furniture, and the place probably needs 60,000 dollars in repairs. But I'll get there. I can't wait to show it to you."

Libby tried to remember when she had ever seen him so happy. Nothing came to mind. "Wow.

You've done really well, Tony, I'm glad. All your dreams are coming true."

"Not all of them, Lib. But I have high hopes. So what can we do for you?"

Libby handed over the folder she was carrying. "I definitely want the Sunday insert. And depending on the budget I would like a daily."

Tony was quiet while he flipped through the couple of pages she had given him. "This looks good... Dolce-McKay?"

Libby shrugged. "I think it's catchy. Plus it capitalizes on my Italian training... Dolce is *sweet*."

"It is catchy." Tony nodded. "We can definitely do this. You are working out of your mom's kitchen?"

"For now. I haven't given up on the dream of my own café, but one step at a time."

"Sounds like a good plan. Ready to go?"

"What?" Libby was surprised when Tony stood up.

"To the wine festival? You still want to come with me, right?

"Of course. But we haven't really talked about prices, and I …"

"Don't be dumb, Libby. There's no charge."

"Absolutely not! You have a business to run, and I have a budget—including advertising funds."

Oops. He'd insulted her. She was sometimes easier to talk to in emails. Having to see her in person tended to scramble his brain, making him say things wrong. "I didn't mean that, Libby. I wanted to help. I tell you what." He handed her a half-sheet sized card. "Here's our ad contract. All the prices are listed. I insist on a 25% friends and family discount. It's what I offer your mom when she runs coupons. Now, whether or not you make up that 25% in cookies is entirely up to you."

Libby visibly relaxed.

"Now come on." Tony slung a camera bag over his shoulder, and held the door open for her. "Let's go have some fun."

They did have fun. Booths and tents crowded the fair grounds, and at one end of the field a band was playing for a handful of picnickers. Most of vendors were selling wine, but there were also food tents, and a few crafts and novelties stands. Music from the band filtered up to them and Tony took her hand in his as they began weaving around, checking out the various displays. Despite that he was on official business, Tony seemed to genuinely want to ensure Libby was enjoying herself. He carefully asked her opinion on each of the wines they sampled, expertly coaxing her to share with him the basics of wine tasting. He must be a very good reporter, Libby supposed.

"Now we picnic," announced Tony brightly, when they had seen just about everything. Libby backtracked a little to purchase a demi-bottle of a light rose wine she had particularly enjoyed. She blanched when Tony reached for his wallet. Not that she had chosen an expensive bottle, but it wasn't the cheapest she had seen either. "Relax," he admonished when he saw her face. "You're a tax deduction—I am taking a consultant out for drinks." Tony winked as he accepted his change and handed Libby the bag.

"Okay," Libby agreed. "What should we eat?" She headed off towards the food venders.

"You choose. I would have no idea what food to pair with what wine."

"That's the beauty of a rose wine—it goes with just about anything."

She ended up ordering a crusty baguette, and some cheeses.

"Tax deduction, remember?" Again, he refused her offer to pay. "I should have brought a blanket," Tony lamented, looking down at her cream colored pants.

"Afraid of a few grass stains, Marchetti?" Libby challenged lightly.

They ended up down by the bandstand, side by side on the grass with their small picnic between them. All around them couples and families were settling down now that the evening was drawing closer. An older couple was sweeping a waltz across a tiny dance floor, and a few children were playing ring-around-the-rosie.

"Who would have thought to bring kids to a wine festival?" Tony chuckled as he watched them flouncing dramatically into grass each time they finished their song.

"It's not the same as bringing kids to a bar." Libby chewed thoughtfully on her bread. "Wine isn't really about drinking. It's more about experiencing."

Tony arched an eyebrow at her.

"It's true." Libby swatted him playfully. "More traditionally it is about experiencing a meal, but the philosophy lends itself well to life."

Tony nodded. He looked impressed. "Okay—so they will have memories of a picnic and music, even if they are having juice boxes?" He gestured towards the children.

"Yeah, and their parents will have memories of watching them laugh and play. Benjamin Franklin said, '*Wine makes daily living easier, less hurried, with fewer tensions and more tolerance.*' And I think Thomas Jefferson called a good wine '*a necessity of life.*'"

"I like that." Tony withdrew a small notebook from his camera bag and started scribbling.

"Umm… I'm not sure I got it exactly right."

Tony shot her a look. "I'm a pretty good fact checker." She hoped she hadn't insulted him.

When he finished writing, he stood up decisively and pulled out his camera. "Time to earn a living!" Snapping photos as he walked amongst the picnickers, Tony captured families playing together and lovers dancing. Libby sat sipping her wine and watching him work. Every so often he stopped to speak to someone, or have them sign what she supposed was a photo release. He moved easily, laughing with people as though they were old friends or fading away discreetly as couples snuggled back into each other's company. Eventually he turned and strode back to where she was waiting for him. Raising the camera again, he took several rapid fire shots of Libby still lounged on the lawn. She laughed and raised her now empty glass in a salute to him. Lowering the camera, his eyes found hers, and his expression seemed to be full of desire. But that just goes to show what an afternoon of consuming wine will do to your perceptions.

The rest of the evening passed enjoyably. Touring the tents and booths one more time, Libby stopped to admire a display of jewelry; in particular a pretty blue crystal strung on a long chain. Immediately Tony handed over a few bills and lifted the necklace over her head.

"I don't think this is a tax deduction," Libby joked to cover her discomfort.

"Nah, the paper isn't paying for this. Consider it a thank-you gift for schooling me in all things vino."

It was hands-down the best non-date Libby had ever had, she reflected later that night as she lay in bed remembering and committing every moment of it to memory.

Chapter Fifteen

"I hate Med School."

"Well, I guess it's a good thing *you* aren't in med school." Libby propped her phone between her ear and shoulder so she could listen to Mel complain and mix at the same time. Stuart wanted Biscotti to sell at his concession stand, so she was hijacking her mother's commercial kitchen in the evenings after the bakery had closed. It was probably nepotism, but Libby knew better than to look a gift horse in the mouth.

"Oh. You know what I mean. John is hardly ever home anymore, and I'm pretty busy too. We never have any time to—you know. It's been almost a week."

"Jesus, Mel! I am so sorry you haven't gotten laid in a week."

"Oh well. It isn't like it's your fault." Mel either missed, or disregarded, Libby's sarcasm. "I'm really looking forward to this weekend though. John promised not to bring any textbooks with him."

"Are you two going away?"

"Yeah, didn't I tell you? It's the family reunion. You should come! We never get to see each other even though we are in the same country again. You can defend your title in the pie eating contest." Libby used to go to the Marchetti family reunion every year. When Mel hit puberty she started bringing boyfriends instead.

"I was 14 the last time I went to one of those things. I am sure that over the last 8 years somebody else has won the pie eating contest."

"Sure, there is always a winner. But no one has ever cleaned 7 pie plates since you."

Libby remembered how proud she had been that year. At fourteen she hadn't realized yet that cleaning 7 pie plates was less than ladylike. "Okay, yeah, if you think it's okay with everyone I would love to come. But no promises on the pie eating contest."

Libby was forming the biscotti when Tony came through the swinging door that led from the front counter to the kitchen. As though the last two years had never happened, Libby found herself back in the last moment they had been alone together in this bakery. As clear as if he were still whispering in her ear, she heard, *Hard and fast between your mother's ovens?* It was really a good thing she wasn't still in love with Tony, or this would be awkward, Libby thought as she concentrated on the dough in front of her. When had she flattened it?

"Hey, Lib. Your mom let me in on her way out."

Tony leaned back against the wall and watched her shape a loaf of dough. For such small slim hands they sure seemed strong. Kneading and patting, her fingers seemed to move with a sense of purpose. What wouldn't he give to be that lump of dough? Why did he always seem to be fixating on Libby's hands? If he had enough blood left in his brain for thinking he would probably be ashamed of himself.

"Are you listening to me?"

Damn. "Sorry, Lib. My mind wandered. What did you say?"

"Never mind. What did you need?"

Need? Tony actually took a step towards her, and her hands, before he was able to shake loose the control his hormones had on his motor functions. Slow, that was what she needed. Time to get over the Italian chef, and then Tony would amp up his game.

For now he would be content with a few dates, and with showing her how great they could be together.

"I just wanted to stop by and invite you to a party this weekend. Actually, it's the Marchetti family reunion." Why was she looking at him that way?

"I know… I just told you I was going with Mel and John."

Stupid hand fetish. "Right. Umm… well, no telling when those two will drag themselves out of their hotel room. Why don't you let me pick you up? You don't want to risk missing the pie eating contest!"

Tony's eyes twinkled at her. Geez, why was everyone so focused on pie lately? "Okay, when should I be ready?"

Once they'd made arrangements for the next weekend, Tony pulled up a chair and found a pen and a pile of napkins so they could play tic-tac-toe while her loaf thing was baking. She beat him 28 games to 3. But to be fair, he was a bit distracted. She had a way of holding that pen…

"Don't fill up, Libster! The pie eating contest is after lunch! I'm gonna give you a run for your money." John barked out his laughter. Libby wondered briefly if it was wrong to hope that he drop his chilidog down his shirt. Of course, Mel was sitting in his lap, and she didn't really want to listen to Mel complain about her ruined tank top the rest of the afternoon, so Libby guessed the chilidog solution was probably out.

Libby had dressed carefully that morning. A short pair of green shorts and a bright blue tee shirt that fit closely and had a V neck designed to show off a small amount of cleavage. She knew the day would probably be too hot to leave her hair down, but she did anyway. Her dark curls tumbling down past her shoulders were a nice contrast against the blue of her shirt. So she snapped a ponytail twister around her wrist (in case she came to her senses later) and left her hair loose. Libby tried not to think too hard about why she was putting so much effort into her appearance. When not thinking about it failed, she settled on the idea that she had been noticing Tony for 15 years, and it wasn't wrong to want him to notice her back. Noticing didn't do anybody any harm, after all.

Tony did indeed notice her when she answered the door. In fact, he was bothered for a good while as to whether or not her shorts actually qualified as clothing. The park was a little more than an hour from Taylorsville, and that was a long time for him to spend not staring at her tanned toned legs. Legs that he would love to have... NO. This was only their second date, and he was going slowly. 'Going slow' became a mantra that Tony repeated over and over to himself for the rest of the day.

When they arrived at the party, Tony took Libby around to introduce her to any family she hadn't met, and the ones that she hadn't seen in many years. There were a lot of '*Oh, I remember you*'s, '*This couldn't be little Libby McKay*'s, and to Libby's great mortification there were even a few mentions of pie. That was mostly the aunts and women cousins. The men were more prone to offering Tony winks, nudges and suggestive handshakes. His cousin, Nick, went so far as to slug Tony's arm and refer to him as a sly dog. Tony preened like a peacock.

Seeing Libby here with his family pulled at his heart. A feeling so tender it left him speechless. His thoughts seem to naturally drift a few years into the future and to bringing Libby to one of these things as his wife, and maybe as a mother. What would their babies look like? Dark curly hair, he decided. Whatever else, he wanted a baby girl with dark curly hair.

"Libby McKay!" Frankie jogged up to them. "How the hell are you? Hey, Tony. You aren't gonna deck me if I shake your hand, are you?" Tony glared at his cousin, but he shook his hand anyway.

"Come on, Lib. I think I see Mom and Dad." Tony towed Libby away, and behind them she could hear Frankie hooting loudly.

"What was that all about?"

"I hit him once a few years ago, and he likes to bring it up." Tony slung an arm around her shoulders a little possessively.

"Oh." Libby had a sneaking suspicion that she knew exactly when Tony had punched Frankie.

Pie eating wasn't the only game on the docket for the day. The Marchettis were very competitive. A large official looking white board was standing in a corner of the pavilion; it served as a schedule of activities as well as the signup sheet. Libby had loved the games as a kid. It was just her and her mom, and now Stuart. That wasn't nearly enough people for egg tosses, relay races, and scavenger hunts. Libby remembered Tony as being less than enthusiastic about the games—well, except for the softball game that brought the party to a close each year. But when Libby reached for the marker at the signup sheet, he gamely added his name next to hers for the three-legged race, water balloon toss, and of course for tug of war.

The three-legged race was the big Marchetti opener. A chalk dust sprayer had been used to mark off a 30 yard race.

"I'm planning on winning, McKay. Don't let me down." Tony was grinning her favorite grin as he tied the scarves around their ankles and thighs. If she didn't know better she would think that he lingered down there a little longer than was necessary.

"Oh, we are so going to own this." Libby pretended to polish her fingernails on her sleeves.

The thing about three-legged races is they don't really rely on speed as much as teamwork and balance. Libby and Tony got off to a pretty good start. His arm held her tightly around her waist, and she put her hand on his shoulder. This would have been perfect to keep them balanced if Libby could have disregarded the tiny jolts of electricity bouncing around in her stomach brought on by his closeness. They kept pace until about halfway down the track. When Tony's fingers slipped between the waist of her shorts and the hem of her tee shirt, digging momentarily into the bare skin at her waist, Libby lurched in reaction. Tumbling forward, Libby inevitably took Tony down with her.

His arms wrapped around her in an effort to absorb most of their fall, but really only served to lock them together when they hit the ground. Tony's face fell into the curve of her shoulder; his body aligned perfectly with hers. Lavender assaulted his senses, and for just a moment, or maybe two moments, Tony wished they weren't in a public park surrounded by his family.

"Are you okay?" he asked, staring down into her eyes.

"Nothing wounded but my pride." Libby was blushing scarlet. Tony rolled quickly away before the sight of her flushed beneath him could cause a problem.

By the time they untangled themselves, the winners (an aunt and uncle Libby didn't recognize) were doing a mildly obnoxious victory dance. The Marchettis really were very competitive.

"Gee, I hope you guys do better in the water balloon toss!" Mel was waving from the sidelines with John standing behind her both hands wrapped around her waist. As Tony had predicted, they had shown up well over an hour late. Libby was glad Tony had offered to bring her or she would have missed a big chunk of the party.

"Hey, sis, John." Tony walked over to hug his sister and shake his future brother-in-law's hand. "Are you going to join us in the water balloon toss?"

"No. Way," Mel exclaimed. "I wore white," she explained in a loud whisper.

"Where do we sign up?" John waggled his eyebrows in a way that Libby supposed he thought was sexy—it was actually a little gross.

"John!" Mel swatted at him playfully, and in return he swung her over his shoulder fireman style.

"Those two should come with an adult content warning." Libby shook her head at them.

"Singing to choir, Lib. Remember, she's my *sister*!" Tony made a retching motion with a finger down his throat.

The four of them watched the rest of the games for a while. Cheering for Nick when he came in first place in horseshoes, and for John in the relay race (even though John didn't do particularly well).

In the water balloon toss, teams of two stood across from each other tossing a water balloon back and forth. If the balloon broke you were out, and if it stayed intact you took a step back and tried again. Tony may not have been enthusiastic about the games, but he was just as competitive as the rest of his family. Right up until the start whistle blew he was muttering instructions to her. "Soft hands, don't squeeze, throw underarm…" It was extremely annoying, and Libby clapped along with the rest of the crowd when Tony burst their balloon in the third round.

"So much for *soft hands!*" Libby yelled to him as he peeled off his now wet tee shirt.

Libby had to remind herself that she was no longer in love with Tony. Because if she had still been in love with him, the sight of him elbowing his way out of that shirt, and the sunshine gleaming off his very well defined chest, would have been enough to make her swoon.

In retaliation to her taunting, Tony stole his neighbor's water balloon and beamed Libby in the back with it. This of course resulted in water balloon anarchy, and soon there wasn't a dry Marchetti in sight.

Tony produced a picnic blanket from somewhere and laid it out on the ground. Libby stretched out on her stomach, letting the sun dry her shirt. Good thing she hadn't been wearing white.

They lay there quietly for awhile. This was one of the things Libby loved about her friendship with Tony. They never felt a need to fill silence.

When they did talk, Tony asked her opinion on a few story ideas, and then Libby showed Tony how to make poppers out of dandelions. By the time the call went out for tug-of-war they were both dry and dressed again.

Tug of war was always men against women. You would think that would be unfair. But the Marchettis were very heavy on the estrogen and the girls' team easily doubled the number on the boys' side. Park regulations kept them from digging a traditional mud pit in the middle of the rope. But they had instead filled an inflatable kiddie pool with what looked like whipped cream. Where would someone purchase that much whipped cream? Geez, these people did take their games seriously. Libby made a mental note to remember to bring a change of clothes next year. And then she made a mental note to remember that she probably wouldn't be there next year since Tony was not her date.

The men did win, but Libby managed to stay clear of the whipped cream—so it was a personal victory in light of a team loss.

"Are you sure you want to skip the pie?" Tony asked her after they had finished lunch.

"Positive. A lady does not consume multiple pies in one sitting."

Tony pictured her for a moment with fruit and whipped cream smeared across her mouth. It was a damn shame that Libby was a lady. "Okay, well then let's go watch at least. Nick's pretty good. He's my bet."

"I would take that bet. You forget I have seen John eat. The year Mel burnt the turkey? John must have polished off three pies... and that was just for fun. Now his reputation is at stake!"

"You're on." Tony leaned against a post in the pavilion. There were no chairs left so he tugged Libby's back into his chest and settled his hands at her hips. So much better than chairs. "What would you like to bet, McKay?"

"Cookies?" Libby suggested, wondering if her voice sounded normal.

"Nah. Mine still suck; I would be too humiliated to pay up if I lost. I tell you what—we'll play for a movie. You win and I will watch some sappy musical with you, and if I win you have to watch The Matrix with me."

"High stakes. I don't suppose I could steer you away from Keanu Reaves? Or perhaps persuade you to make a switch—Bill and Ted's Excellent Adventure?"

Tony wondered if she had any idea the images she inspired with words like *persuade.* He was reasonably sure she could persuade him to do just about anything. "Not a chance."

Nick and John both lost. Tony declared they would compromise with a Die Hard Marathon.

"Ball time!" someone bellowed from the baseball diamond.

"Let's go." Tony tugged Libby towards the softball game.

"I'm just going to watch."

"No way, you gotta play. This is the best part!"

"I'm not playing. I don't even think I know all the rules."

"I forgot, you don't like team sports. Do you remember when you tried out for cheerleading?" Tony shook his head at the memory. "Okay—let's take a walk then."

"No, you go play. I will watch—and cheer," Libby teased.

In the end Tony did not play ball. He wanted to, but today was about Libby. So they went for a walk instead. There was a path through a small strip of woods. And if Tony remembered correctly there was a creak with a pretty little bridge over it. Holding her hand, Tony strolled slowly down the path. The trees were thick enough that it was darker and quieter than the open area of the park. In fact, it was downright romantic. Tony stopped thinking about the missed softball game.

"What's that?" Libby pointed into the trees above them.

"I believe that is the rare red-bellied-long-tail-wood-swallow!" Tony deadpanned without looking up.

Libby snorted and nudged his chin up with the tips of her fingers.

"Oh, *that*," Tony said as if only just then realizing his mistake. "That looks like a kite." Perched just above them, a plastic looking kite was lodged in the tree limbs.

"Give me a hand."

Libby was already scrambling up the trunk. Tony hoisted her higher and tried not to stare at her ass… much. It took a little while for Libby to reach the kite, and then another few moments to untangle what was left of the string. For a few horrifying seconds Tony was sure she was going to come crashing down.

"Look out below!" The slightly battered kite floated to the ground and Libby began inching backwards on her branch. "Umm... I think this is going to be harder on the way down than on the way up."

Tony stood beneath her, calling instructions and warnings. Soon she was shimmying back down the trunk. "I gotcha." Tony reached out to grasp her waist the moment she was within reach.

Twisting as she dropped the rest of the way to the ground, Libby ended up in Tony's arms with her back pressed to tree trunk. Oh, this was so much better than softball! Tony closed the remaining distance between them. One of his knees pressed between hers; inhaling slowly, Tony enjoyed the lavender smell of his Libby. Carefully, Tony pulled a twig from her hair, and cupping a hand along her cheek he leaned towards her—

"What's that?" Libby was startled out of moment.

Sure enough, they began hearing whispered voices: "There's a stream with a bridge just a little further down this path," Tony's cousin Nick was saying as he came into view around a bend. He had one arm wrapped tightly around a blond girl in a pink sundress, and he was nuzzling her neck as they walked.

Tony straightened up, pulling away from Libby. It almost killed him, but a gentleman didn't allow his date to be caught groping in the woods. He waved a little as Nick and his girlfriend passed, but he wasn't sure they even noticed.

"Sounds like Nick has big plans," Libby joked as she smoothed her clothes and hair.

"Yeah, he's real original," Tony responded edgily. "Should we see if this thing still flies?" Tony bent down and scooped up the kite before leading Libby back into the open park.

Chapter sixteen

It had been a month since the Marchetti Family Reunion. Mel and John's wedding was a little more than two weeks away. Orders had begun flying into the bakery for Dolce-McKay, and Libby was on cloud nine. It seemed that everything in her life was just as she wanted it. Just about. After the family reunion, Tony started coming around a lot. Not that that was really a problem, because Libby loved being with him. They never seemed to run out of things to say to each other, or things to laugh about together. But being so close to him, and having him look at her the way he had in the woods at the park—it was confusing. She didn't want to be in love with Tony— well, she was pretty sure she didn't want to be in love with Tony.

As agreed, Tony organized a Die Hard marathon. They ended up in Stuart's family room, because Tony didn't have living room furniture yet. And somehow Libby found that endearing. Some days Tony would come by the bakery with lunch for two, and once she had renewed her membership at the Y Tony started joining her for morning runs a few days a week. Last week Tony had driven her to the beach, and they had built sandcastles. Being with Tony was becoming an awful lot like breathing—absolutely necessary.

"Man, do I have news for you!"

Libby always enjoyed when Mel called—she could almost hear the italics in her friend's voice.

"What's that?"

"Guess who I just spoke to on the phone—no, you will never guess—and he's calling you next."

"Then I guess you better spill."

"Gio!" The name almost exploded through the telephone. "Libby? Hello?"

"Gio? My Gio?" Libby was speechless. Why on earth would Gio be calling Mel? They had written a few letters and emails since Libby had left Rome, but he hadn't exactly inundated her with transatlantic phone calls. To be honest, she had pretty much figured that Gio had forgotten or changed his mind about visiting America or about trying to pursue any type of relationship with her. What had she thought? That he would pack up his life and move just to be with her?

"How many Gios do we have in common?"

"To be honest, I didn't think any… why have you been talking to him?"

"He's coming to the wedding!"

Libby dropped her phone. "Sorry—what?"

"I sent him an invitation. It was just a lark really—who would have thought he'd say yes? Girl—he must have it bad for you! You totally downplayed that accent!"

"Call waiting, Mel! Gotta go!"

It was him.

Libby was glad Gio was coming. He had hired a new manager for the restaurant, and classes at the culinary institute were finished for the term. He had laughed at her surprise that he was planning a visit.

"Betta! We talked about this. I said I wanted to see America, and I do. I want to see you. I have cleared my schedule, and I can stay at least a month."

Libby wondered what *at least* meant.

Gio arrived a few days later, on a Friday morning. She met him at the airport, and true to her memories, he was devastatingly beautiful. Also true to her memories, being with him had a surreal quality. They actually ran into each other's arms in the airport. Well, they walked quickly towards each other, but Gio did scoop Libby off her feet for a kiss worthy of any sappy romantic movie. It was a little embarrassing actually, because people were staring.

"Have you missed me, Betta?"

"Of course, Gio!" And she had. It wasn't Gio's fault that she hadn't had time to dwell on how much she missed him.

"Is something the matter?"

"No. No. It's just—you know—the airport—people are looking at us…"

"Ah. Do you think Gregory Peck would not have kissed Audrey Hepburn in an airport?"

"Gregory Peck was the American," Libby corrected him. As if pointing out that dissimilarity discounted his point. They had watched Roman Holiday together many times last year. In the movie the hero was American, and the damsel was European.

"Sorry about…" Libby waved her arm out the glass door, indicating where it was cloudy and wet outside. Libby hated that it was raining. Some time the night before, a steady drizzle had soaked the ground and coaxed a bunch of worms out of hiding. Normally rain didn't bother Libby, but she felt bad that Gio's first day in America would be so dismal.

He was laughing at her. Libby had almost forgotten how often Gio laughed at her. Also that she found this habit slightly annoying.

"The sun should be out the rest of the week," Libby added defensively.

"Ah—Mia Betta. Apologizing for the weather?" He was still chuckling softly as he dropped a kiss on the top of her head. "I have missed you."

Libby decided to forgive him for laughing at her.

Gio wanted to get checked in at the hotel and rest after the flight. Libby felt a twinge of guilt that she hadn't invited him to stay at Stuart's. Her mom was away teaching a pastry workshop and Stuart had driven up to spend the weekend with her. She felt weird enough staying there alone, but alone with Gio? It would be a bad idea. So they made plans for Libby to pick him up after lunch and she would show him the bakery. Mel and John were also coming in tonight. They would be staying with her parents for two weeks while they saw to the final details of the wedding. Mel desperately wanted to be at the airport when Libby picked Gio up, but she had been mollified by a promise that they could all meet up later that evening for drinks at a local bar.

Gio loved the bakery. Libby's mom loved Gio. So that went well, she supposed. Next they drove around the town. They saw Libby's old high school and the park where she and Mel had played as kids. Libby didn't know why she felt strange showing Gio this part of her life. He certainly didn't seem bored. He was full of questions about her childhood, and then about what she had been doing since she returned from Italy, about her catering business. And then he was full of advice on new locations for when she was ready to try opening her own shop. Libby wasn't all together sure she enjoyed having reality elbowing its way into her European adventure.

Later that night, when they met up with Mel and John, Libby relaxed a little. She liked the bar. It wasn't any of the ritzy clubs Gio had taken her to, but it wasn't a dive either. Libby had been here a few times over the last few weeks, and she liked it. The band was always good enough for dancing, but not too loud, and the drinks were reasonably priced. Libby thought things were going pretty well. Gio seemed to get along well with her friends—even John.

"Right! The European adventure!" John exclaimed with his usual lack of tact when Libby introduced him, as he reached across the table to shake Gio's hand.

Gio merely arched an eyebrow in Libby's direction before grasping John's hand. "I guess that would be me."

"Ignore him, Gio. Everyone else does," Libby had muttered.

"Congratulations are in order?" He changed the subject easily by nodding to where Mel was sitting next to John. "And my best wishes to the bride." It was the perfect tactic. Mel was off a mile a minute about the wedding and how she had always wanted to be married on the beach. If Mel wasn't already charmed by him at that point then she was completely won over when he ordered a round of champagne to 'toast to her happiness.'

"He is just yummy, Lib." Mel was touching up her lip gloss in the ladies' room. "And a great dancer. I do love a man that can dance."

Gio had obligingly twirled Mel around the dance floor when John proclaimed himself much too sober to make a fool of himself. Not that John didn't dance; he was just more of a shuffler whereas Gio had spent the early part of the evening spinning and dipping Libby with practiced expertise.

"Yeah. He's terrific," Libby agreed.

Mel twitched a look at her in the mirror. "You aren't mad that I invited him, right?"

"No. Of course not. I am glad he's here," Libby protested

"Okay, good. Because I can tell he adores you." Mel turned around, snapping her hand bag shut. "Tony is going to drop by," she mentioned not so offhandedly.

This was a pretty big surprise. Libby hadn't seen Tony since Wednesday, when they went out for ice cream. That was when Libby told him that Gio was coming into town, and Tony had been acting sorta weird ever since. She'd gone back and forth between hoping it was jealousy and being irritated since he had long ago forfeited his right to be jealous.

Tony had made it very clear what type of relationship he would be interested in—and Libby wasn't interested.

"Good. That's good he can meet Gio."

Back at the table, John was fervently trying to convince Gio of baseball's superiority over all other sports. Libby recognized the quirk of a smile on Gio's face, and knew he was more amused than anything else by John. Maybe, she thought, Americans were funnier than she had realized.

When Tony walked through the door, Mel waved widely over her head to get his attention.

"Gee, I'm so glad I found you, sis, in this sea of people," Tony teased as he surveyed the half empty room.

"Ha ha, very funny." She swatted him, and pulled out a chair next to her for him to sit down. Tony ignored her and pulled out the chair on the other side of Libby.

For some reason this introduction was more awkward. Actually, Libby knew the reason, but she pushed it aside and tried to act normal. The funny thing about acting normal is that you have to be a really good actor.

"The chef," Tony acknowledged as he nodded deeply.

"The writer." Gio's voice was gruff.

"That's right. My third novel just made the bestseller list." Tony was clearly going for a practiced, bored tone of voice, but his excitement won out.

The table erupted in conversation. Mel and Libby threw their arms around Tony in a three-person hug, and John hooted his congratulations. Grinning and laughing, Tony was saying how he had known it was a possibility, but he'd just gotten the call from his agent that morning and it was low on the list, but *on the list* was all that mattered. With a flick of his hand to the waitress, Gio ordered another round of celebratory champagne. Later John would end up drinking Tony's untouched glass.

"Mia Betta. You have very talented friends."

"I do indeed." Libby was too full of pride for Tony to take notice of Gio's change in demeanor.

"What did you call her?" Mel gushed from her end of the table.

"It's my name in Italian." Libby shrugged, blushing. "Gio says everything sounds nicer in Italian."

"It isn't *only* her name," Tony muttered, so low that Libby was able to pretend she hadn't heard him.

The moment was quickly swept away as Mel demanded an impromptu Italian lesson. Gio politely supplied her with translations of any and all phrases she could think of. "He's right! Everything does sound nicer!" Her eyes suddenly got wider. "John! Let's do our vows in Italian! It would be so romantic."

"Anything you say, babe, but it might be nice if our families were able to understand what we're saying. Hell—I'd kind of like to understand it myself. Plus I already learned the English ones."

Mel's face fell a little.

"I'm sure your ceremony will be lovely just as you have planned," Gio said somewhat absently.

"You're right, of course." Mel cheered up "Isn't this just like old times, Libby? Us hanging out on a Friday night? I feel like we ought to be singing *Under the Sea.*"

"Let's not, and say we didn't, hmm?" Libby glanced around the bar and wondered how much her friend had had to drink.

"Of course not, silly. It is too bad though that my parents don't have a guest room anymore. We could have had a sleepover, and you wouldn't have to go to Stuart's alone." Mel pointed her eyes in Gio's direction in a not so discreet fashion.

Libby thought she preferred sleeping alone in Stuart's house to being a part of a sleepover that included John. "I'll be alright."

"I have a suite at the hotel," Gio murmured in a low voice. "With a lovely pullout couch in the sitting room," he added when he saw what must have been sheer panic on her face.

"I have a guest room," Tony all but shouted. He calmed down a little. "You could stay in my guest room, Libby."

"Don't be ridiculous, big brother," Mel said icily "You don't even have furniture." This brought a raised eyebrow from Gio.

"I have furniture," Tony defended himself. "I just haven't picked anything out for the living room yet." He turned to Libby. "My guest room is your guest room, Lib. And you haven't seen my new house yet. Stay the whole weekend if you want—it will be just like old times." Tony shot a pointed look at Gio.

"Umm. Yeah, maybe. I really didn't want to stay at Stuart's. And—" She turned toward Gio. "I'd hate to crowd you."

Standing up, Libby announced her intention to use the ladies' room. "Order me something to drink if I miss the waitress, okay?" she called over her shoulder to no one in particular.

She did miss the waitress. Which was no surprise since the bouncy blond woman had been back to check on their table every five minutes anytime Gio was seated. When he was on the dance floor, John had taken to walking to the bar for their drinks—it was quicker that way. Of course, the waitress started with Gio—two glasses of the house white—and she barely glanced at the others as they ordered. Tony asked for a glass of water, and a Cherry Coke extra cherry.

When Libby sat back down she found a glass of wine and tumbler of soda in front of her chair. Tony wanted to punch the air and do a victory dance when she reached for the Cherry Coke. His elation lasted only a moment.

"Ballare?" Gio murmured, covering Libby's hand with his own. They shared a private smile and headed for the dance floor.

"Did you know, Betta, I have a friend who owns a restaurant in New York?" Gio held Libby close, moving slowly in time with the music but mostly concentrating on her face.

"Oh? Did you want to take a trip to New York while you're here? We should, you know. It is prettier in the fall, but summer is good too."

"Perhaps." Gio studied Libby in a way that made her want to fidget. As if he was trying to come to a decision. "My friend, Elaine, she lives in New York now, but spends her winters at home in Italy. I have been thinking lately that I could adjust my schedule in a similar way. Perhaps six months here, and the fall and winter in Rome?"

Libby stared at him, a little dumbfounded. "You want to spend six months out of every year in New York?"

Gio took a deep breath. "No. I was thinking perhaps of North Carolina. I thought you would enjoy wintering in Rome."

Realization dawned on Libby. Gio wanted them to be together. Here and in Rome. Certainly she would say something—just as soon as she remembered how to breathe.

"Ah, Mia Betta. I never had a chance, did I?"

Libby was still too busy forcing air in and out of her lungs to manage an intelligent reply. "Hmm?"

"Against Big Brother over there, I never really stood a chance, did I?"

"What? No, of course you did—do! Of course you do. It's just, that is a big change for you to make, and I'm not sure... I do want to be with you, Gio."

"No, Betta. I think you want to want to be with me." Gio kissed her lightly and leaned his forehead against hers. "We could have been fabulous together, you know?"

Libby sighed. "I just think we might need some time..."

"I thought so too. I knew someone here still had a hold on you, but I admit that I had hoped the distance and time would have proven insurmountable—for him. It is alright. I see the way you look at each other, and I want you to be happy."

"Tony. He doesn't see me that way," Libby admitted quietly.

"I think, then, that he is an imbecile." This made Libby laugh. "Do you remember meeting my Nona?"

"Of course." The previous Fall, Libby had been unable to shake homesickness. Rome was lovely, but no one celebrated Thanksgiving. Gio brought her to his grandmother's house. Where Nona had cooked a full Thanksgiving dinner. Of course, she served baked ziti and bruschetta along with her turkey, but Libby was really an it's-the-thought-that-counts kind of person.

"Did you know she was only married to my grandfather for 16 months before he was killed?"

"How awful."

"Don't let her hear you say that." Gio smirked a little. "Nona figures she knew more love in those 16 months than some people ever know in all their lives. She says she is lucky. And she never remarried— she says some loves are forever."

"That's lovely. Sad, but lovely," Libby whispered, thinking of Nona living on memories all those years.

"It is the kind of love I want to find for myself. I think I will go to New York. In the morning."

"Tomorrow!"

"Si. I have four weeks off and I said I wanted to see America. I will come back before I return to

Italy. And then I think we will be fabulous together—as friends."

"Thank you, Gio." Libby didn't know what else to say.

"Thank you, Betta, my American adventure. Come. Let's get his attention, shall we?" A twinkle lit up Gio's face.

"You want to help me make Tony jealous?"

Gio chuckled, and spun Libby in a wide arc before pulling her back to him. "Tony and every other man in the room. Did you not know that I have been the target of much jealousy this evening?"

The rest of the night passed without much incident. Gio continued to provoke Tony lightly, and Tony continued to bristle at the words *Mia Betta.* But all in all they had a good time. When Gio excused himself, commenting that he was still tired from his flight, Libby walked him to the door and hugged him tight. "See you in month?"

"In a month." And with a kiss on her cheek, he left.

Chapter Seventeen

Soon after Gio left, Mel and John followed. "Ready, Lib?" Tony asked in a quiet, almost sullen voice as he stood up.

"Oh." Libby remembered agreeing to stay in his guest room. "Umm, yeah. I think I'll just go home to Stuart's though."

Tony shook his head. "You've been drinking, which means you're riding with me. And my car is headed home. Let's go."

Tony knew full well that Libby hadn't had anything to drink in hours, and that Stuart's house was more or less on his way home so he could have dropped her off there. But he wanted her to himself. He had hated sharing her with Gio all night. *Go slow* indeed! He was such an idiot. He should have met her at the airport with a minister in tow. Now he had to compete with Italy's answer to *Dancing with the Stars* in person instead of just the memory of her European fling. Not that he was giving up. No way. He would fight as hard as ever.

Tony fumed inside his head all the way to the car, and the entire drive back to his house. He hated Gio! Hated. Mel had mentioned he was older, but come on! The guy was ancient! And the way he pawed at her all night! Always touching her arm, or brushing nonexistent hair out of her face. It was positively disgraceful. Tony had barely contained the impulse to grab Libby and run as fast as he could towards the door when he first heard Gio whispering *Mia Betta* in a lover's voice. Mia, as in mine. Well think again, pal, Tony thought, Libby has been mine for years... she just hasn't realized it yet. She would though. Tony just needed to find the right way to show her. How could he convince her?

"So... are we here?"

Tony realized they had pulled into his driveway, and he wondered how long he had been sitting there spacing out. "Oh, sorry, Lib. Guess I'm tired. Yep. This is it."

Tony and Libby had to run for the door. The drizzle from the morning had turned into a shower, and then into a downpour, and now it looked to be progressing toward thunderstorm.

Tony's house was a pretty stone Victorian. There was a small covered porch with a white porch swing to the left of the front door. It looked like a home, Libby thought. Inside, Libby looked around and burst into giggles when her eyes rested on the living room.

"And I thought you didn't have living room furniture!" Libby teased as she plopped down into a plastic lawn chair. One of four set up in the otherwise empty room.

"Well, I didn't want to brag." Tony lowered himself into another chair and stretched dramatically. "I will get furniture," he continued more seriously. "And with this news about my book, money shouldn't be a problem anymore."

Libby nodded sleepily. "That's great, Tony. You don't have to defend yourself to the girl living in her stepfather's sardine can-sized guest room. Show me the rest!" She popped up out of the chair.

The kitchen was a warm affair with a big island and it opened into an equally warm morning room. The baker in Libby noticed the ample counter space, and double ovens. This was a dream kitchen. Unbidden images of Tony wearing a pink apron and shoveling cookies into his mouth sprung into her mind.

"Can I get you anything? I have juice, and not much else." Tony poked his head into the fridge. "Sorry. I eat out a lot. There might be some lemonade mix around here." Tony rummaged through empty cabinets as if sliding their meager contents around on the shelves would produce more appetizing choices.

"I'm good, Tony."

Libby wandered around the two rooms. She liked them. She liked the house. There was something distinctly intimate about being here alone with Tony so late at night. It reminded her a little of late night Monopoly games—only the feeling was a thousand times more powerful. And then she realized something—it hit her with a crash! Actually, the crash was thunder outside, but the effect wasn't lost on Libby. Standing there dripping slightly onto the tile floor and watching Tony foolishly worry about beverage choices, Libby realized that she was Nona. Tony had ruined her for all future romance. Not even hot Italian chefs who adored her and were willing to rearrange their entire lives for her were capable of swaying her heart. She was going to be in love with Tony for the rest of her life. Damn.

"Well, I promise to make it up to you with the best take-out breakfast we can find in the morning." Tony abandoned his search and turned to find Libby staring thoughtfully off into nowhere. "You look tired. Want to see your room?"

"Okay." Libby numbly followed Tony up the carpeted spiral stairs. Charming, she thought. Just like the rest of the house, and just like Tony.

"Well, this is the bathroom—there's another in the master so you can have this to yourself, and my room is that door there." Not that she needs to know that, Tony chided himself. "And this is you." Tony swung the door open to reveal a guest bedroom that was furnished with his childhood furniture from the Marchettis'.

"No wonder your parents don't have a guest room anymore," Libby teased, taking a step into the room.

Something wasn't right. What was that noise? They both saw it at once.

"Shit!" Tony rushed forward, feeling the bed. It was soaked. And there was a steady drip coming from the ceiling above. "Oh man!" Tony moaned as he pulled the bedding back, revealing the soaked mattress beneath. "Know any good roofers?" he joked lightly over his shoulder.

"Sorry, no." Libby shook her head. "Is it very awful?" she asked.

"Not as bad as it could have been. The bed is trash, but it probably saved the floor. And I knew the roof needed work. I have just been too busy to look into it. Guess I should have made time." He shoved his fingers through his hair. "Okay. Damage control." He jogged out of the room and returned with a big sheet of plastic and a large pot. They pushed the bed out of the way, and put the plastic drop cloth in its place to protect the floor if the pot didn't catch all the drips. Afterwards Tony carried the bedding down to the laundry room.

Having done all they could, Tony and Libby stood staring at each other in the hallway. Because now there was one bed.

"Sorry about this, Lib. Listen, you take my room. I'll…"

"Sleep on the couch?" Libby finished for him with a smirk.

"The floor, I guess." Tony grimaced at the idea.

Libby knew the obvious solution was to ask him to take her back to Stuart's. But something else had been niggling at the back of her mind since her epiphany in the kitchen—she wasn't really Nona, because Nona had 16 months of happy memories. So if Libby was doomed to spend the rest of her life alone, she was damned sure going to have at least one memory.

"Can't we share?" Libby hoped she sounded sultry. She didn't have much call for *sultry* in her life, so she was sort of making things up as she went. "I mean, we are both adults and old friends... I am sure we can share with no *problems*." Okay, now she was getting sultry confused with slutty. But she was getting desperate, so maybe slutty would work. Besides, Tony had only ever been interested in her as a casual partner—maybe slutty was good? No, she had some pride; slutty was out.

Tony's throat went dry. So did his brain—all the blood seemed to have deserted his brain. How much had she had to drink? Did she have any idea what she was saying? Tony tried to think back and count the hours since her last glass of wine. He hadn't had anything but water all night. He had been punishing himself by living through all those *Mia Betta*s stone sober. He was pretty sure that it had been several hours since the wine—pretty sure, but not positive.

"Tony?"

"We can share. I guess that would be okay." He couldn't do it. Well he *could* do it. Physically he was definitely able. But you don't take the woman you love to bed for the first time after she's been out all night drinking, not to mention dancing with another man. Of course, that was tonight. Tomorrow was a different story. "Umm, wait here."

Tony rushed into the master bedroom. Libby heard a few clunks and bangs. He was straightening up for her! So very charming.

"Okay. That's as good as it's gonna get." He popped his head back into the hall.

Walking into Tony's bedroom made Libby's stomach flip. It was so very like those nights when they had been teenagers playing Monopoly. Except they weren't teenagers anymore, and Tony's parents weren't asleep down the hall, and they didn't have a Monopoly board.

"Nice," Libby commented as she took the master bedroom in. The bed was big and sort of made. She had a feeling he had thrown the covers up just now. A big picture window looked down over his backyard, or it would if it weren't so dark outside. A door that probably led to the master bathroom was on one wall, there were a few dark wooden dressers lined up against another wall, and matching nightstands framed the bed.

"Yeah, it's nice." Tony wanted her to love it. He wanted to tell her he had bought it for her—the bed, the dressers, the whole damn house was for her.

A part of his campaign to win her over; show her that he could give as much to her as any Italian chef.

"Tony?"

"Yeah?"

"I don't have anything to sleep in."

"What?"

"Your car was only headed home, remember?"

"Oh right." He had been kind of an ass at the bar, but he had been looking forward to having Libby to himself—and then she had mentioned going back to Stuart's. So yeah, he had been an ass. He could have at least stopped and let her pack a bag. "Do you want to borrow a tee shirt?" He would never be able to sleep if she was lying next to him wearing only his tee shirt. Not that he planned on being able to sleep anyway.

"I have a camisole on under this... Maybe if you have a pair of boxers or something?"

"Sure, here you go." Tony numbly walked to a dresser and tossed her a pair of blue boxers. He wondered what a camisole was. Some kind of undershirt, he guessed. He pulled extra pillows out of the top of the closet, and started lining them up down the middle of the bed. "Umm… just in case," he muttered when she raised an eyebrow at him.

Of course. Libby's insides came crashing down. Clearly she had no idea what was slutty, sultry, or otherwise. He was determined not to take advantage of her, and she was too mortified to be any bolder. So much for her one memory. "I guess I'll just use the bathroom, and get changed."

Dejectedly, Libby walked into the hall bath and changed clothes. Hanging her dress over the bath tub to preserve it for the next day, she walked back into Tony's room.

Okay, not an undershirt! A camisole was apparently a torture device made from silk and lace. Tony could barely tear his eyes from Libby, she was so beautiful. Her camisole was beige (practically skin colored) and scraps of lace teased at the tops of her breasts. Breasts that were obviously bare beneath that silk. The material pooled slightly at the neck line, and Tony wondered what he might see if she were to lean forward slightly.

"I'm gonna grab a shower." A cold one. "Don't wait for me or anything." Tony walked right into his bathroom and didn't look back.

Officially a failed seductress, Libby climbed onto her half of the bed, careful not to destruct the great wall of pillows, and fell asleep... eventually.

Tony took a long cold shower. And then he waited, he counted to a thousand, he folded the pile of clean towels in his linen closet, he cleaned the toilet, he tried to remember all the states in alphabetical order (he could only think of 47—wait, North Carolina—48!), and then he quietly eased into the room, slipped into the bed, and waited for sleep. *6 times 8 is 48, 7 times 8 is 56, 8 times 8 is 64.*

Chapter Eighteen

This was his best dream. Tony was dreaming of lavender, and silk, and soft, soft skin. In his best dream ever, Libby was spooned in front of him, her silk covered breast filling one hand, and her hip curved temptingly beneath the other. Of course, normally in his Libby dreams she wasn't wearing shorts, but no matter; he tugged the cotton down low enough to gain access to a palms worth of warm smooth skin. Dream Libby made a soft mewing noise. Tony's eyes flew open. Libby, real Libby, was curled into him. Her soft perfect bottom nestled into his hips, and her legs tangled with his. Craning his neck slightly, Tony could see a pile of pillows lumped near their feet. Who had moved the pillows? Duh. He was the one on the wrong side of the bed. Libby mewed again.

Tony tried not to panic. He also tried not to think about the incredible sensations awaiting him if he were only to thrust forward slightly. Lesson number one in how to send a woman screaming into another man's arms: Molest her in her sleep. What the crap was wrong with him? Slowly, gingerly, he eased the elastic of her borrowed boxer shorts back into place. She was still lying on one of his arms. Holding his breath and praying she stayed asleep, Tony cradled her in a loose hug and rolled their bodies until he was able to slide his arm free. The loss of her weight and warmth against him pierced painfully in his chest. His arms wanted to reach out and pull her close again, so he got up and stalked into his bathroom for another cold shower.

Twenty minutes later, and wondering at the ineffectiveness of cold showers, Tony tiptoed quietly back into the bedroom. He didn't so much as glance towards the bed. His body was demanding that he climb back in there and finish his dream. Maybe he should get out of here? Breakfast—he owed her the best take-out breakfast he could find. Tony remembered his promise from the night before. A course of action began to take form in his mind. He would slip out and bring back a big pancake breakfast. She probably had some plans or another with the chef later today, but he would make the most of their morning together. Plan in place, Tony crossed the room to his desk, intending to leave her a note in case she woke up before he returned with the food. A tiny noise and a bit of movement at the edge of his vision stilled him at the foot of the bed.

Turning, Tony saw Libby—eyes still closed, she had flipped onto her back, the sheet and blanket kicked down to her waist, and the outline of one hand was unmistakable underneath her camisole. Riveted to where he stood, Tony felt his body tighten almost painfully. A groan escaped him before he was able to get control of himself.

Suddenly fully awake, Libby opened her eyes. Embarrassingly aware of the position Tony had caught her in, she closed them again.

"Morning, Lib." Tony's rich voice floated over her. "Watcha doin'?"

She dared to peek at him. His face was hungry and lustful. Of course, she thought, he had always been attracted to her body. It was her heart he had no use for. "Umm... I had a dream," she hedged.

"I guess you did. Wanna tell me about it?" Because I bet I was having the same one, he added to himself.

No way, thought Libby. No way was she going to admit that she dreamed of being wrapped in his arms, of his morning stubble scratching the side of her face while he was leaned over her hair inhaling deeply. "Gio. Of course I was dreaming of him."

Tony saw red. "In my bed! You were lying in my bed... doing what you were doing, thinking of another man!" He stared at her, daring her to change her answer.

"Umm... I ..." Libby was shocked into action. She scrambled backwards on the bed a little. Why had she said that? She could have just refused to answer. Insulting him was not the way to get him to join her in bed. She only wanted to convince him that she wasn't looking for emotional attachment and that she could handle no-strings sex. She wanted him to let himself give her that one memory she had longed for all night long. Surely now he would throw her out of his house.

"Well, I guess I know what I have to do." Tony reached out and wrapped a hand around her ankle, yanking her back towards the end of the bed. "I am going to show you what you should be dreaming about. Sweetheart, I am going to love you until you can't even remember Chef Boyardee's name." He climbed onto the bed, stretching his body over hers, and took her mouth in a long thorough kiss. "We aren't getting out of this bed until I have driven every thought of every other man out of your beautiful head."

"Okay."

Tony began to fulfill his promise by kissing a trail down her throat, his tongue sweeping across her skin, capturing every delicious inch of her. His hands smoothed down her stomach until they grasped the hem of her top, dragging it upward until he had revealed her perfect rosy topped breasts. Molding his hands over them, Tony moved his oral assault lower, licking a path to one peak, where he laved a tight nipple with his tongue while rolling the other between his thumb and forefinger. Her body arched and writhed beneath his, begging for more attention. He obliged by repeating the process in reverse.

Libby felt each nerve ending explode with pleasure, and at the same time she was straining for more. Hot and hungry need was building in her chest. She tried to content herself with touches and tastes of his skin, but he ruthlessly evaded her attempts. "Let me, sweetheart," he commanded as he pressed her back into the bed. "Let me make you feel good. I can be so good to you." He was almost muttering to himself as he resumed.

Worshipping as he went, Tony used his tongue and hands to press every button he had ever discovered, read about, or even just imagined on a woman's body. There wasn't a spot of unloved skin on her body. He peeled his boxer shorts and her panties off her body, tossing them carelessly to the floor. "You are so beautiful," Tony whispered against her skin as he scattered kisses around her bellybutton. "I knew you would be."

Slowly, he lifted one leg, and starting with her ankle he worked his way up, paying special attention to the skin behind her knee. When he reached the place she most wanted him, he shot her a teasing smile as he skipped right over the apex of her thighs and began his trek down her other leg. Finally satisfied that he had tasted all of her—well, almost all of her—Tony returned to that most intimate place. His tongue flicked over her. She moaned. Masculine pride surged through him. He was making her make those noises. He had reduced her to unintelligible pleasure-filled mutterings. Tilting her hips to give him better access, Tony suckled and nibbled his fill of her delectable skin.

"Please," she begged above him.

He could tell she was close. "It's okay, sweetheart. Just let it happen," he urged her as he redoubled his attentions.

Release washed over her like waves in the ocean—incredible, pleasure giving waves. "Oh, Tony." She breathed out as she came back to earth.

His name. His bed. His Libby. His name. His bed. His Libby. A fog of lust rolled through Tony's brain when he heard her moaning his name.

"Don't move," he ordered. Reluctant to leave for even a moment, Tony stretched out towards his nightstand, and after some rummaging he returned to her with a foil packet. That taken care of, Tony captured her mouth in another kiss. Hot and demanding, this time Tony tangled their tongues together as he grasped her thighs and thrust into her.

Beneath him, Libby cried out into his mouth. Tony became still on top of her. Pain glittered in her eyes where desire had been a moment before. "Libby?" Tenderness rushed through him. She had trusted him with something so precious. "Why didn't you tell me? I would have been more careful with you."

"Anymore careful and I would have fainted from the want of it all," Libby whispered as she kissed his jaw.

He remained still, unsure of how to proceed, terrified of hurting her more, but unable to withdraw.

"Tony?"

"Hmm?"

"You know how to do this, right? I think one of us should."

Tony chuckled softly. "Of course, sweetheart—It's just… I don't want to hurt you, Libby."

"Oh. Okay. Well, you're not hurting me." Tony looked at her doubtfully. "Really," she insisted, "it only hurt for second." Libby wiggled her hips experimentally.

Tony growled and buried himself deeper. With long methodical strokes, he began building them towards a slow sensual peak. When she shuddered beneath him, moaning his name again, all semblance of control deserted him. Faster and faster he possessed her, taking from her all the things his body needed. Finally, after groaning out her name, he collapsed on top of her. Rolling to his side to avoid crushing her, Tony gathered Libby to his chest and pressed breathless kisses to her face and hair, and anywhere else he could reach.

"Wow," Libby managed sometime later.

"Are you okay? I'm sorry I got a little… erm, enthusiastic at the end."

"I liked enthusiastic," Libby purred into his chest hair. Awareness swamped her, and she realized that now she could do all the touching and tasting that she'd missed out on. Her fingers scratched tentatively along his abdominal muscles. Relishing the hardness of his body, Libby grew bolder in her caresses, wanting to please him as he had pleased her.

"Wait." Tony stilled her movements, trapping her small hands in place on his stomach with his own.

"Did I do something wrong?"

"Not possible, Lib." Tony pressed a quick kiss to her mouth. "I can't tell you how I have longed to feel your hands on me. But we can't try this again just yet."

"Oh, right. I knew that." Libby nodded. "Umm, Tony? How much time?"

"What?"

"How much time, until you are... 'Til you can..." She trailed off when he started laughing.

"I meant you, Libby," he said. "You are probably going to be... well, sore."

"I am totally willing to risk it... You know—when you're ready." Libby smiled at him.

Tony tugged Libby's hands lower and showed her just how ready he was.

Chapter Nineteen.

When Tony woke up, the clock glowed 11:00 am. He hadn't slept away an entire morning since college. Although he hadn't done that much sleeping this morning either. Libby was snoring lightly next to him. God, she was beautiful. He wanted to wake her up. Maybe with a kiss? Maybe with something else.

His stomach growled. He was too hungry for the something else, and Libby was bound to be hungry when she woke up too. Quickly Tony slipped out of bed, pulled on fresh clothes, and after leaving Libby a note on the nightstand he left in search of the very best take-out breakfast (or lunch) he could find.

Libby's favorite diner was only ten minutes away. There would be a lot to talk about when he got back, and he wasn't above bribing her with a stack of pancakes. He was going to convince her that he could make her happy. He was going to show her that she belonged with him, in his life, in his house, and in his bed.

"What did you do!?" Mel screeched through the phone while Tony carried enough food for an army back to his car.

"Good morning, sis!"

"Don't you try that charm on me, buster! Where is Libby?"

Awkward. Could he tell his baby sister that her best friend was asleep in his bed after a long morning of lovemaking? No. "Umm… she's still at my house, Mel. I went out get us break—lunch."

"Don't tell me! I don't want to know. You have gone too far. I never thought you could be so low. Although, after your spoiled brat display last night I don't know why I'm surprised."

"Want to tell me what's bothering you, Mel?"

"Gio is gone. Whatever you and Libby did last night, they must have had a fight because he checked out of the hotel. I hoped he'd come to his senses and decided to stay at Stuart's with Libby— but Stuart's was empty and her car is still at the bar. So that means she was with you last night."

"What's wrong with that?" Gio was gone? Had she called him? Told him to leave?

"Nothing if I thought for a second you were serious, but we both know you're not. You are usually a pretty stand-up guy, Tony. I don't know why you keep stringing her along this way. Gio loves her! He was going to move here, you know. He told me last week when I talked to him on the phone."

"He was?"

"Well, that or she was going to move there… it was confusing, but he had plans."

Tony had plans too. "He wanted her to move in with him?"

"To marry him, big brother. I am sure he was going to ask her to marry him. I definitely got a wedding ring vibe. You can't stand to see her happy with somebody else, can you? You are such a selfish ass! You don't love her, but you want her to keep on loving you? She loves Gio, Tony. I could tell just from the way they danced together."

Marry her? They hadn't even slept together. Unless maybe she had been waiting for the wedding night? Some cultures were still kind of serious about the whole virginal bride thing, right? Tony wanted to scream. He wanted to say that he had loved her since she'd cleaned him out in Monopoly six years ago. But that was not the kind of thing you said to a girl's best friend before you said it to the girl. He settled for, "I care a lot about Libby."

"No, Tony, if you cared about her you would have wanted her to be happy. Whatever! I am going to try her cell again."

"No. Mel. I am two minutes from home. I will talk to her. Promise me that you will stay out of it... Mel? Hello?" Damn. Tony sped up. Mel was wrong. Libby couldn't be in love with Gio—she just couldn't.

Waking up a little achy and gloriously satisfied in Tony's bed was the best experience of Libby's life. Well, anyway—it was definitely up there. Libby reached for Tony. But he wasn't there. Pulling her camisole back on and his boxer shorts, Libby went to find him. Except he was really gone. After checking the house, Libby peered out a window and found his car was gone. He had just left her there. Curling up right on the living room floor, she let the sadness have her.

Tears slid down her face. How could she have thought she was prepared for this? That she could handle being a *just sex* kind of girl if it meant she could be with him. She was wrong. She wasn't a just sex kind of girl at all. Parker was right, and now she had probably blown even being his friend. Because she knew that she could never again be satisfied to be with him without actually being with him.

"Libby?" Tony called as he rushed through the front door. "Libby…"

She was crying, curled up on the floor, because he hadn't even had the time to buy furniture. What was she doing down here anyway? Maybe she hadn't been able to stay in his bed after her fight with Gio. Mel was right. She must love him.

"Libby, sweetheart, please don't cry." Tony dropped the food in the hallway and went to hold her. She was probably feeling guilty. Guilty because she had been seduced by Tony when it was Gio that she really wanted.

"Don't worry. Look, I talked to Mel, and I know Gio left. Did you have a fight?"

"What? Oh. Not a fight—a sort of a disagreement." That was a little true; they had disagreed on their future. There was no reason Tony needed to know that she'd been slightly relieved when he'd decided to go. Libby wiped her eyes with the back of her hand. "I'm just being a silly girl. I'm going to get dressed, and then maybe you can drive me home?"

His heart fell like a rock. All remaining hope that she might have chosen him fled. She didn't want him, and he was only making things worse for her by pushing. Mel was right, he was a selfish ass. "Your disagreement? Was it... did you tell him about last night?"

"What? No. I haven't talked to him since he left the bar." Libby slumped into Tony, and tried not to think of the irony in Tony consoling her for a broken heart he had given her.

Last night? She and Gio had fought last night? Libby slept with him on the rebound? And now she regretted it. Now she wanted him back.

"Okay, well. Listen, I am sure that things will work out. You don't need to tell him about... you know."

Libby cried harder.

Tears pricked at the back of his eyes. It was so hard not to beg her to stay, to beg her to forget Gio. But if she was this miserable now, Tony knew she could never be truly happy with him, and he couldn't live his life waiting for Gio to turn up and steal her back from him.

"I'm so sorry, Lib. If he loves you it won't matter—and if you're still worried just… maybe you can just fake it? Go real still and gasp or something."

"What?" Libby lifted her head to look at him.

"I mean if you're, umm… if Gio was expecting… on your wedding night?" Gee, for a man who made a living with words he was doing a hell of a job stringing a sentence together now. "What I am trying to say, Libby, is that I want you to be happy. So I am going to back off. I'll stop calling, and taking you out. And I swear Gio will never know that we dated. If I have to have Mel's tongue cut from her head—he won't find out."

Shock forced Libby to finally hear the words Tony was saying. But she was still really confused. "When were we dating?"

Tony's eyebrows crumpled together. "You know… before. The past six weeks."

She was still staring at him.

"The picnic, and the wine festival, and all those lunch dates. We wasted an entire afternoon on Die Hard!"

"Mel invited me to the picnic. And the wine festival was about for the paper. They weren't dates—you never said they were dates. Die Hard is never a waste! "

If it wasn't so awful, Tony would have laughed at her. Really? Was now the time to continue their John McClain pissy or not pissy debate? "Of course they were dates—what did you think we were doing?"

"Hanging out, I guess. A date would be different—getting dressed up, you picking me up, bringing me flowers, taking me out to dinner or dancing or…" Libby's face fell.

Shit. He had forgotten the flowers. Now that she mentioned it he was pretty sure Mel had mentioned flowers at some point. "I forgot about the flowers, and I didn't think you wanted to go to a dressy meal. I would have taken you anywhere you wanted."

"You're right," Libby said quietly. "We were dating." She dropped her head into her hands and moaned.

"I'm sorry, Libby." Tony didn't even know what he was apologizing for anymore. But this was the first time he had ever made a woman cry just by taking her on a few dates. "Maybe they weren't dates?"

"No. They were." Libby kept her face down. It was hard for Tony to read the expression on her face when all he could see was her hair. "Tony Marchetti finally takes me out on not one but several dates—and I missed it."

"Libby? I am seriously confused here."

"Me too."

They sat there for awhile holding each other, neither one sure what to say. Finally, Libby broke the silence. "What wedding?"

"Hmm?"

"You thought I was going to marry Gio? You mentioned a wedding night."

Tony looked very uncomfortable. "Mel seemed to think that's where things were headed."

"Mel's dumb."

Tony allowed himself to feel relief, and hope. "You aren't then?"

"No. Gio and I decided to be friends."

"And you're okay with that?" Libby nodded into his shoulder. "Then… why did I walk in and find you crying on the floor?"

"Oh. Sometimes girls cry?" Libby looked at him hopefully. Maybe he would let her get away with that. He stared back. "Okay, I just realized that I am not a *just sex* kind of girl. When I woke up alone my feelings were hurt that you would just leave like that. But it's okay."

"I was coming back! I didn't want to wake you. Didn't you read the note?"

"There was a note?"

Libby's cell phone rang. Tony picked it up. "Stay out of it, Mel!" He hung up on her.

Tony squirmed away from Libby slightly so they were sitting facing each other. He couldn't have this conversation if he was distracted by the smell of lavender and sex.

"Do you remember me telling you once that we have communication problems?"

Libby nodded.

"Okay. So there is some stuff I need to know. Are you in love with Gio?"

"No."

"You don't want him back?"

"No."

"Why did you let me believe you were sleeping with Parker?"

Libby looked embarrassed. "I didn't want you to think I was pining away over you."

Tony looked pained. "I am an ass."

"Is that a question?" Libby started to smile.

"Nope. It is plain old fact. I'm in love with you. I have been since—well, it's been awhile. And I am hoping to God that you love me too."

Libby's jaw dropped open. And then she smiled, crawled into his lap, and kissed him.

"Oh no, you aren't getting off that easy." Tony grinned her favorite only-for-Libby grin. "I want to hear you say it."

"Of course I love you Tony. I'm Nona."

"Nona? Care to explain?"

"Maybe later." Libby took another kiss. "Where did you go then?"

"Oh. I brought breakfast," Tony mumbled absently as he shifted her more fully into his lap.

"Food? I'm starving!" She crawled out of his lap towards the forgotten bags by the door.

"Thrown over for cold pancakes!" Tony gripped his heart as though he'd been wounded. This was his Libby. And she was—really his.

All the food was reheated, and Libby got her promised take-out breakfast—at 2:00 in the afternoon.

"I think we should get married," Tony announced mildly from his side of the table.

Libby spit out her pancakes. "Married?"

"Yeah—we suck at dating." Tony's smile broadened across his face. "We can move you in here today. And I know you weren't sure about staying in Taylorsville, but I can write from anywhere. There's a paper in Tallahassee that was pretty interested in me before, if you want to go back to Florida. Or if you still want to try New York, that's cool."

"When did you talk to a paper in Tallahassee?"

Oops. Busted. "Before you went to Rome. I missed you, Lib. I didn't want us to be apart anymore. I still don't want us to be apart. What do you say? Marry me? I promise to buy you any sofa you like."

Libby just stared at him. Maybe he had miscalculated.

"How long?"

"Until we can get married?" Tony hurried over to her side of the table.

"No. How long have you been in love with me? You said it was *awhile*."

"Oh. Umm, it's kind of embarrassing. You were still pretty young."

Libby tossed him an exasperated look. "I'll tell you if you tell me." Tony nodded. "Okay, don't laugh. It was the day we met. You stole our popcorn and made fun of The Little Mermaid."

"That describes most Friday nights of our childhood, Lib." Tony's tone was light. "It was the summer we played Monopoly. You were wearing those tiny blue pajamas, remember? I had to sit in that awful desk chair just to keep from pinning you to the bed—which I probably could have been arrested for since you were only 16."

"You were only 19! Is age always going to be an issue with you?"

"I guess that depends on if you are going to marry me."

Libby took another bite of her pancakes. "I love it here. I want to stay, and I think my mom can handle the competition. We cater to different crowds really. We can pick out a couch later if you want."

"Libby!" Tony shouted. "Communication, remember? Will you marry me?"

"Isn't that what I just said?"

"The words, Lib. I want to hear the words."

Libby grinned "Yes, Tony. I will marry you."

Tony swept her up out of her chair and headed for the stairs. "We can pick out the couch later," he said as they crossed into their bedroom.

Epilogue

Four years later....

Mia Betta,

Elaine and I thank you so much for your gift. We were sad for you to miss the wedding, but it is good you don't travel in your condition. Please congratulate Tony for us on his newest novel. I am afraid Elaine is quite besotted with Isaac Raines.

We shall be back in New York in a few months and we cannot wait to meet the newest Marchetti. Please tell young Luca that his Uncle Gio says it is a very special responsibility, being a Fratello.

Perhaps next year you can bring the family to Rome? Nona would love to see the children.

Love,

Gio

More Works by T.J. Dell
Saving Face
Smile For Me
Whispers in the Woods (The Elfkin Series)
A Dog Named Jingle Bells

For more information and for upcoming release dates find T.J. at Facebook.com/dell.tj

Made in the USA
Lexington, KY
29 November 2012